MAID MACHINEGUN　Aaliyah

MAID MACHINEGUN Aaliyah

Maid Machinegun

A NOVEL

Aaliyah

Illustrations by Suzuhito Yasuda
Translated by Anastasia Moreno

BALLANTINE BOOKS · NEW YORK

A Del Rey Manga/Kodansha Trade Paperback Original

Maid Machinegun copyright © 2006 by Aaliyah
English translation copyright © 2008 by Aaliyah

Published in the United States by Del Rey Books, an imprint of The Random House Publishing Group, a division of Random House, Inc., New York.

DEL REY is a registered trademark and the Del Rey colophon is a trademark of Random House, Inc.

Publication rights arranged through Kodansha Ltd.

First published in Japan in 2006 by Kodansha Ltd., Tokyo, as *Maid Machinegun.*

Library of Congress Cataloging-in-Publication Data

Ariya (Novelist).
  [Meido mashingan. English]
  Maid machinegun / Aaliyah ; illustrations by Suzuhito Yasuda ; translated by Anastasia Moreno.
    p. cm.
  ISBN-13: 978-0-345-50253-7 (pbk. : alk. paper)
  I. Yasuda, Suzuhito.   II. Moreno, Anastasia.   III. Title.
  PL867.5.R59M4513 2008
  895.6'36—dc22

                                            2008000467

Printed in the United States of America

www.delreymanga.com

9 8 7 6 5 4 3 2 1

Translator: Anastasia Moreno
Cover illustration: Suzuhito Yasuda
Text design: Caron Harris

Contents

MAID MACHINEGUN Aaliyah

Welcome Home, Master

Hmm . . . Today, I need to order two bags of lemons, three packs of cream, and one bag of crème fraîche. After mopping the floor and polishing the china, I was completely exhausted. Back in the break room, I pulled off my white-brimmed, frilly headband, kicked back with a cup of tea, and turned on my laptop.

Greetings. My name is Aaliyah Kominami. I work as a waitress in a small café in Akihabara. To be more precise, it's a maid café, where the waitresses all dress in traditional maid uniforms. Our café is a tiny flower blooming in the vast garden of Akihabara. Unfortunately, we aren't at all well known. All the other maid cafés have gotten lots of magazine and TV coverage, but we've been pretty much ignored. A Master with a maid café blog visited our café several months ago, but we haven't had any interviews since. Actually, his website was shut down immediately after the interview, so we never even made it onto his blog. Does *anybody* know about our café at all?

B-But, I won't lose! Even if I'm about to!

Today, I started a diary on the Boiled Eggs Online website to tell potential Masters about our wonderful maid café. I hope the seeds of this little project will grow, first into large trees, then into large forests, and eventually cover the entire world! Even Doutor and Starbucks will have maid waitresses! McDonald's bestselling menu item will be a Teriyaki McMaid Burger! You'll see a maid on the right, a maid on the left, and a maid in every direction! The goal is to have a billion maid cafés around the world! The Cabinet's most influential position will be the Maid Minister! You'll tell a friend who's down on his luck to "go to a maid café if you want to feel better! ★"

W-Wait, I'm not a preacher!

Er, ahem. Umm, I just want to promote wonderful maid cafés, that's all. Besides, shouldn't a visit to the maid café be part of your itinerary while in Japan anyway? With a bit of courage and curiosity, you'll experience Paradise, Dreamland, and Shangri-la! You'll be missing out on life if you pass up such an opportunity. What percent of life's pleasures will you miss? A hundred percent, of course. In other words, the value of your life will be reduced to zero! The true reason behind the origin of life on Earth and space can be found in maid cafés. The divine truth is found here. All theories are proven here. Everyone please yell, "Maid cafés rock! Maid cafés will eradicate absurdity! Off to the maid cafés, the maid cafés, the maid cafés . . . !"

I swear I am not a preacher!

Er, I have a feeling some of my Masters will shy away after reading this . . . b-but, I just got a little carried away, you know? Well, I knew I deliberately repeated the word "maid" at least twenty-one times thus far, so I hope the subliminal effect created a growing urge for you to go to a maid café. Yes, I'm sure of it! I can brainwash my readers if I repeat the word enough times.

Though there are a large number of Masters who believe that going to a maid café is just as important as breathing air, I'm also aware of a few shy Masters who probably think, *I want to go to a maid café, but it's a little intimidating.* Don't worry! Today, I prepared a quick introductory course for prospective Masters. If you pay attention to what I have to say, you will be able to visit maid cafés without any problems. Knowing yourself and your enemies will make you a fearless warrior, and earn you a hundred victories!

MAID CAFÉ 101

First, you need to know where to go. Look for a maid café in your area. Akihabara used to be the only place with maid cafés, but these days, they're all over Japan. Do an Internet search, or go to the local bookstore and vociferously demand a book on maid cafés! The bookstore employees will probably look at you funny when you buy the book. And if you actually jumped around in the shop like a wild maniac, then you shouldn't ever go back there. Once you gather enough material, try to find a maid café that grabs your attention. Of course, you might be tempted to go to a maid aromatherapy spa, a maid massage parlor, a maid cabaret, or a maid game center, but before you jump into those variations, you should try the standard maid café first. Once you do that, then you can explore the other possibilities.

Once you find a maid café to your liking, your next step is to pack. Oh, you don't need a lot of money. Prices in maid cafés are comparable to those in regular cafés. You can enjoy a lot of tea, food, and maids here. I assure you . . . you will definitely get more than your money's worth!

Okay, so after finding the right place and preparing for the big adventure, you are now standing in front of a maid café. If you're a shy Master, I'm pretty sure you're blushing and quite nervous, but please calm down. Take a deep breath and regain your composure. If that doesn't work, think back to the toughest moments of your life. That awful day someone put tacks in your gym shoes at school . . . when your mother threw away your almost-completed *Ganpura* . . . that time you bought a newspaper subscription you didn't really want because it was the only way to get rid of a pushy door-to-door salesman . . . and so on. Okay, so these memories are probably depressing you, but it's okay, you'll be comforted soon enough. The ideal formula is: "I want to die" level depression + maids = comfort. The deeper your depression, the greater the comfort the maids will give you.

You're now ready to enter the maid café!

Please imagine your favorite voice actress saying to you, "Welcome home, Master. ★"

Upon entry, a row of cute maids will welcome the return of their Master. Let the happiness begin. At this moment, you will truly be grateful to your parents from the bottom of your heart for giving birth to you. You'll feel like you're at the top of the world. But be careful! Just because maids are nice, don't assume they'll play down-and-dirty games with you to fulfill your beastly desires! You'll end up eating cheap pork rice bowls or soggy ramen noodles sharing a table with an old man who's cosplaying as a lunchbox at a lame state affairs café. Remember, have fun within established limits. It might sound like an oxymoron, but this is a key concept in maid cafés.

"This way, Master. ♥"

Before you know it, a maid will show you to a table. Please follow her quietly. When you're seated, she'll bring over a glass of water. The water's free, of course. Please drink some water, relax, and browse through the menu at your own pace. You'll probably notice a wide variety of food, drinks, and desserts on the menu. Getting lost in the menu is part of the fun. Please take your time. Oh? Did you notice a special service written next to each menu item? You're quite observant. This is what makes a maid café so special.

For example, next to the *omu-rice* . . .

"A maid will draw a picture on the omelet with ketchup. ♫"

Did you decide what to order? Wonderful!

Try to get a maid's attention. Since this is your first time here, you might be reluctant, but please make an effort to call for a maid. During busy times, maids might not notice you immediately, but please don't feel you're being treated like an outcast. Don't worry. You belong here. Please call out a few more times, just a little louder. The maids will notice you soon.

"Have you decided, Master? ★"

See, a maid finally responded. After you order promptly, just sit back. It's normal for many of our Masters to "come home" (patronize the café) alone, so you won't feel lonely at all. Please feel free to read a book or play with your laptop while you wait for your order. You can also just sit and look at the maids. Randomly catch a glance or two, or just ogle all you want. If you are a seasoned Master, you might even strike up a delightful conversation with one of the maids, but until you've reached that point, you shouldn't try too hard, or you might keel over from nervousness. If you die from a heart attack, your parents would be sad in so many ways.

"Thank you for waiting, Master. ★"

After a few minutes, a maid brings your order of *omu-rice*. She has a bottle of ketchup in hand. The maid will ask, "What shall I draw?" Please tell her to draw a picture, mark, symbol—whatever you'd like, really.

I suppose you could make a hard-core fanboy request like . . .

"Dhalsim's facial expression when his Yoga Fire was countered with a Dragon Punch."

. . . but I'm sure the maid will only giggle. Maids are very kind and gentle, so they won't show how troubled they are with your complicated request. Please don't trouble or tease the maids too much. Please ask her to draw something simple, such as a heart or "Welcome Home. ♥" After you eat the *omu-rice,* your tummy will be filled and your heart warmed. And by then, you will be totally hooked on maid cafés.

But wait!

What did you take out of your bag? Why are you pointing your cell phone camera? Please read the signs in the café!

"No photos inside the café."

Yes, most maid cafés won't allow you to take pictures inside (with very few exceptions). If you're caught taking pictures in a restricted café, then a maid will shoot you dead. . . . No, I mean, a maid will scold you. Don't try to sneak a picture, either. In my opinion, sneaky Masters should be forced to sign a contract with a foreign mercenary unit and sent away (like *Area 88*). Join the *Pineapple Army*. Become a military pawn. Carry a large rucksack and march for four days straight without any sleep. I hope a commander will force a pile of nasty rations down your throat! Or that you'll be punished for being a lowly peasant who didn't declare his utmost reverence to the Holy Mother!

. . . Er, ahem. I repeat, you're allowed to have fun, but within established limits. That's the basic principle to follow in maid cafés. You can have a great time at maid cafés, as long as you follow the rules. After you pay your bill, the maids will graciously send you off, saying, "Have a safe trip, Master. ★" At this point, you have successfully completed Maid Café 101.

So, how was it? If you are itching to go to a maid café, then my mission was successful. I, Aaliyah Kominami, look forward to your return home, Master.

I hope we meet at a maid café! ★

2

Even a Maid's Smile

Can Falter T_T

(Singing like a half-dead zombie . . .): Even maids are human, with real feelings, too. . . . ♬

It's been over a week since my last diary entry. This is Aaliyah. I apologize for starting off on such a sour note. But it was an extremely hectic day at the café, and gosh, am I exhausted!

Our maid café is very small. On weekends, we get hit with wave after wave of Masters, so we rush up and down the stairs all day to please them. Of course, the maids tried their best to please all the Masters, but sometimes, it's just so overwhelming! The bottom line is we don't have enough maids. If it gets too busy, our perfect maid smiles twitch uncontrollably. I seriously doubt that maids' labor rights are protected by federal laws. Maybe there's actually a law that states: "Maids have no rights granted to them"? I sure hope maids are covered by the labor laws, at minimum. If this mayhem continues, then this café will turn into a barren desert, full of dead maid corpses . . .

Argh . . . I couldn't take it anymore, so I protested!

I believe maids have an inherent right to improve their work environment. I heard about the English Tea Strike during the

Industrial Age, where factory workers protested against the reduction of their break time from twenty to fifteen minutes. They insisted, "Fifteen minutes is not enough time to enjoy a nice cup of tea! We need at least twenty minutes to enjoy our tea properly, like human beings!" They won and retained their valuable twenty-minute tea time breaks. Following that example, I believe we shouldn't ruin our Masters' moods by having depressed and overworked maids serve them tea. In order to have maids maintain their pleasant smiles, we need to improve our work environment. Who should I bring my complaints to? The Ministry of Labor? JARO? Or the EOCS? No, I'm complaining to my manager first!

As my blood boiled with righteous indignation, I tensed my shoulders and stormed out of the break room. Our manager, Makoto-tencho, was also dressed as a maid. While she squinted her eyes, filling out complicated logbooks, I vented my frustrations about the distressful work conditions.

"If this dire situation continues, the maids will be worked to death and this pleasant maid café will turn into a 'maid in hell' café. And I can't reach the top shelf, so we need a ladder, too!"

Makoto-tencho didn't respond.

"Umm, Makoto-tencho?"

Though I let loose all my pent-up frustrations about the horrible work environment, she continued to just hunch her shoulders over the complicated logbook in total silence. Oh, wait, she finally looked up and smiled at me. Her eyeglasses glinted as she said, "I'm just going to pretend I didn't hear any of that. ★"

Shouldn't I just whack her with a blunt object?

Makoto-tencho is a very tough nut to crack. Her glasses definitely accentuate her shrewdness. For the most part, she's very amiable and easygoing, but she's a stickler for certain things. She's totally bipolar—she's always making these threats with a sweet but wicked smile, scaring the crap out of us. A while back, she suggested that we "bake our own bread—it's more authentic," so she made the dough herself from scratch. On the other hand, she wanted us to serve instant coffee to "cut back on expenses."

This just appalled me, so I protested, "We shouldn't serve cheap coffee!"

She only smiled back and said, "I don't have time to serve the real stuff because I'm too busy kneading the dough for the bread." Huh? What in the world was she trying to achieve? Better service, saving on costs, or . . . was she just plain fickle?

A-Anyway, it is too early for me to propose work reforms to Makoto-tencho, so I'm backing off for now. But, I'm not running away. I'm advancing to the rear to reorganize my efforts, that's all. "Retreat" is not an option for Aaliyah Kominami!

I returned to the break room to drink tea and formulate a new strategy. Today, I drank the Chinese Lapsang souchong tea. Some people think this tea stinks like *Seirogan* . . . but some tea lovers appreciate its strong aroma. The Lapsang's smoky smell actually sparked an idea. I realized I need something for my strategy to work: allies! One person can't conduct strikes, protests, or student rallies to challenge authority. I need allies to support my cause. There's strength in numbers!

After receiving divine revelation from a cup of tea, I returned to work. Good. I saw Yukino-san sweeping the floor. She's dressed as a butler—a male version of a maid, I guess? She is the reliable, older-brother figure at our café. A while back, she put a perverted prank caller to shame when he asked what type of underwear Yukino-san was wearing. Totally unfazed, she answered coolly, "I'm wearing a tiger-striped thong with gold trim." My hero! But then she didn't talk to me for a week when I started calling her "Tiger Thong Girl." How rude! I was just kidding.

But if Yukino-san would only join my cause, I'd gain the strength of a thousand men!

As she carefully wiped down the tables, I approached her and whispered my strategy so Makoto-tencho couldn't hear: "We're overworked. Someone needs to defeat Makoto-tencho (since I couldn't) before we all die!"

Yukino-san calmly listened to me rant, then replied, "You just need to work three times harder, Aaliyah." Boy, that was *cold*. Ice cold. And harsh. "B-But, if we don't do anything about it, then our maid café will turn into a 'maid in hell' café!"

"Hey, if you have so much time for chitchat, then you have time to clean up the rest of this," she said.

OMG! Best. Comeback. Ever.

Then she threw a rag at me and left the room. My shoulders slumped, and I sighed at the rag in my hand. I was *so* disappointed. Really bummed out. It was hopeless. Is it my destiny to endure such hardships as a maid? Will I just wilt in a corner like a bullied little rookie salaryman, hounded by my evil coworkers . . . ?

"Aaliyah-chan, what's wrong?" a voice called out from behind me.

I jumped and turned around. It was Ruruka-san in a maid outfit. She was polishing the forks in her hand with a rag and duster. I wish she'd stop sneaking up on me like that!

"What were you guys talking about?" she asked, curious about my conversation with Yukino-san. This might be an opportunity to gain allies. But . . . I probably shouldn't tell Ruruka-san about my complaints. Anyone but her . . .

"Hey, what were you guys talking about?" She smiled, as if she noticed my hesitation. Her body language kept urging me to explain. Eventually I surrendered to her oppressive powers and spilled my guts.

Ruruka-san nodded sympathetically and said, "You know, Aaliyah-chan, evil light rays penetrate the Earth's atmosphere, so you need to minimize your exposure to it. Don't worry. You can survive the hexagonal electromagnetic waves by covering yourself with aluminum foil. It'll also block the spiral Adamski spinal receivers.

"You just need to endure the pain until the yellowish-blue hues arrive. Just wait for the golden bug on the underside of a large leaf."

Oh . . . my . . . God . . .

Yeah, um, so, Ruruka-san is this . . . *really* unique person. A mysterious paranoid. Kind of *out there,* if you know what I mean. Okay, she's an unstable nut who definitely belongs in a mental asylum. She has a drug overdose at least once a month. Her hobby is catching cockroaches with chopsticks and then chasing after the kids in her neighborhood with them. She probably said all that about the tinfoil and yellowish-blue hues just to show everyone at the café just how quirky she is. It'd be really scary if she believed that stuff for real, though. Even the wristband she never takes off and the mysterious white pills in her purse are all part of her "persona"—I hope. Otherwise, she's too freaky. And she should stop staring and smiling at the blank TV screen!

In response, I tried to force a smile, but my face twitched. I ran for dear life.

Phew . . .

Back in the break room, I took a deep breath. That whole exchange took the life out of me. It was more tiring than a day's work. I'd so much rather work hard at making my Masters happy than wasting my time recruiting allies for my revolution.

Hmm?

My laptop was still on, even though I was pretty sure I turned it off earlier. So who turned it on then? The text editor was activated, too. And which document was open . . . ?

`Aaliyah_Kominami_Munch_Log.txt`

O-Oh gosh, this was a document I created to log every type of cake I "conquered" (ate) in the café! I swear I hid that file in the deepest confines of my computer, so who dug it out . . . ?!

Suddenly, I heard the door shut in the background.

When I jumped and looked behind me, I saw the "quirky" maid standing in front of the door. She flashed me a wicked smile as she locked the door behind her. Thump, thump . . . slowly but surely, she closed in on me. I was cornered. She stood over me.

No, wait, this was, no . . . s-stop, please . . . st@&qaws#drftgy$jikolp . . . !!

3

Rookie Maid

and Her Steiff Teddy Bear

In our break room was Major Lawrence, a Steiff Teddy Bear. He's about three feet tall, with brown, fluffy hair. I named him "Lawrence" but it was Ruruka-san who awarded him the rank of major. Whenever a maid felt happy or sad, she gave Major Lawrence a big hug. He was our unofficial mascot.

Looking at Major Lawrence brought back memories of my rookie days.

This happened way back in the days when I'd been at the café for barely a month.

I've always been clumsy, and a really slow learner to boot. So at first I was always messing up at the register, forgetting all the menu items, and screwing up when I tried to do more than three things at once. My Masters would just chuckle, thinking that I was playing a "clumsy girl" character. But the more my Masters forgave my mistakes, the more it depressed me.

At that time, a peculiar Master had begun to frequent our café.

He was just this average-looking guy in his mid-twenties. But he *always* came every other day, at *exactly* 2 P.M. He *al-*

ways picked a seat near the entrance, ordered coffee *without fail,* played with his PDA *every single time,* and left in *exactly* twenty minutes flat.

Of course, many of our Masters came alone and brought their own laptops and PDAs, so his behavior wasn't totally out of the ordinary. But he *always* came once every two days, arrived at *exactly* 2 P.M., ordered a cup of coffee *without fail,* and stayed for *exactly* twenty minutes. Everything he did was so mechanically precise that after a while, the maids began to take notice, and the rumors started. What kind of Master was he? Maids aren't supposed to pry and violate their Masters' privacy, but I was way too curious. Anyway, I happen to believe curiosity is just a basic and completely undeniable human instinct.

"Umm, so you always seem to come at the same time?"

"Yes, I suppose."

"I know you enjoy our coffee, but would you like to try some of our tea sometime?"

"Yes, I suppose."

"What's your name?"

"Ozuma."

"Hello, Ozuma-san. My name is Aaliyah. Pleased to meet you!"

"Yes, I suppose."

What a painful, one-sided conversation.

Every time I started a new topic, he answered monosyllabically and slipped away. But even though he gave me such short replies, he didn't seem annoyed. It was pretty weird.

Whenever I served him coffee and returned to the waiting

area, I could feel him staring at me. But when I turned around, Ozuma-san was sipping on coffee and playing with his PDA nonchalantly, as usual. After I turned away and wondered if I was imagining things, I felt his eyes graze me again. Of course, when I flipped around again, Ozuma-san was just toying with his PDA.

But maids have eyes in the back of their heads. I swear to God, Ozuma-san was looking at me!

I explained the situation to Ruruka-san.

"Well, he seems to have a powerful chakra emanating from within," she replied.

. . . Uhh, okay, chakras aside, Ruruka-san was also curious about Ozuma-san. Apparently, he didn't react to any of her quirky little comments at all. Even when Ruruka-san told him, "I am *Amaterasu Oomikami*," he wasn't fazed at all. He only responded, "Yes, I suppose." He's a formidable Master, impervious to our comments.

We kept digging for the tiniest little facts about him, but his identity was deeply shrouded in mystery.

It bugged me so much that I couldn't concentrate on my work. In order to uncover his true identity, I decided to use a maid's ultimate tactic. I knew I shouldn't be doing this, but . . . I followed him out of the café.

Ozuma-san left the café at exactly 2:20 P.M. After much begging and pleading, Makoto-tencho granted me a thirty-minute mid-shift break. I looked at the table near the entrance, and sure enough, Ozuma-san was still sipping his coffee. I rushed into the break room, changed into my regular clothes, and dashed out of the rear exit.

It was Sunday, so the streets of Akihabara were packed with throngs of people. It's a great day to tail someone because I could hide behind any person at a moment's notice. I was an expert on stealth missions (just like *Metal Gear Solid*)! Leave it up to your friendly neighborhood maid detective to watch people night and day from the shadows!

Ozuma-san left our café and walked right into another café. Wh-What an unfaithful Master! I waited five minutes and entered that café, too. I was sure he wouldn't recognize me because I was no longer wearing a maid outfit, and I covered my face with a cough mask and glasses.

"Welcome home, miss! ★"

I jolted at the loud maid voices. I scanned the room to find a seat away from Ozuma-san. Where was Ozuma-san . . . ?

"Whoa, you scared me!"

"Hello, Aaliyah-san."

Ozuma-san sat near the entrance, a few feet from where I stood.

"Umm . . . er . . . well . . . fancy meeting you here!"

"Yes, I suppose."

My stealth mission had utterly failed. I ended up actually *having tea* with Ozuma-san. Gosh, was it uncomfortable! We couldn't keep a conversation going, so we fell silent and just sipped our drinks. Ozuma-san ordered coffee at this café, too.

"Won't all that coffee upset your stomach?"

"Yes, I suppose."

He could have tried to be a little more cordial, but instead he abruptly cut off every attempt at conversation with his trademark monotone answers. Ozuma-san hardened his face. Maybe he didn't like me? Come to think of it, Ozuma-san had seen me screw up so many times in the café that he might not think too highly of me, I realized. I gathered my courage and asked the question.

"Do I irritate you, Ozuma-san?"

"Why do you ask?"

"Wh-Why? Er, it's hard to explain. Do I irritate you because of all the mistakes I make . . . ?"

Ozuma-san silently pulled out his PDA and focused on the screen, like he always did in our café.

He said, "I suppose you make unnecessary movements because you can't foresee the customers' needs. You react too late, so when you try to make up for lost time you become a little hasty and clumsy. Also, you can't be smooth with customers if you haven't memorized the menu, either."

The expressionless Ozuma-san kept stabbing big holes in the delicate fabric of my performance. The other maids usually gave gentle advice on ways to improve, but this was the first time someone put it so bluntly . . . so to be honest, I was completely shocked.

"Please take a look."

Ozuma-san pointed at his PDA. On the screen, I saw that he had painstakingly logged detailed observations of numerous Akihabara maid cafés. Of course, our café was listed, too, and data on each maid were also detailed. As he showed me the data on our café, he stated with supreme confidence, "In my opinion, you're just not compatible with that café."

"B-But, I'm trying so hard!"

"Trying hard isn't enough. You need to show results."

Everything he said was absolutely correct, so I had no way of retaliating. Ozuma-san was a real expert at analyzing maids.

Ozuma-san grabbed the bill and stood up.

"Let's go. This is all the time I need to understand this café."

It was exactly twenty minutes.

When we left the café, there was an air of uneasiness between us. Now that I think about it, what was I trying to find out in the first place? I couldn't even handle my own job, yet I chased after a supposedly "weird" customer. After talking to Ozuma-san, though, I saw that though he might have some quirky aspects, overall he was just a normal customer. His mission was to observe maids with an analytical eye. And Ozuma-san blended in so well in Akihabara's crowded four-way inter . . . Huh?

Oh my God! I'd lost Ozuma-san! To be more accurate, the moment I looked away, he disappeared into thin air. Did he run away because he didn't like me? Or did we just lose sight of each other? I looked around to find Ozuma-san, but there was no way I could find a person in that crowd of pedestrians.

Suddenly, with uncanny timing, my cell phone rang.

Message from: Makoto-tencho

My face went pale. My mid-shift break was over a long time ago! I dashed like a mad maid back to the café.

Not only was I harshly criticized by Ozuma-san, but Makoto-tencho also chewed my butt for about an hour for being tardy. The other maids had to pick up my slack in my absence. I hung my head in shame and almost cried. As Ozuma-san pointed out, maybe I wasn't cut out to be a maid? I brooded, completely depressed.

The next day . . .

Though I greeted my Masters and guided them to the tables as usual, I still felt blue. Whenever there was a pause, I sighed. My smiles were dampened by my depression. With all the hustle and bustle, my shift at the café usually went by fast, but that day just dragged on and on for eternity.

Finally it was 2 P.M. As soon as the wall clock chimed the start of the hour, the door bells clanged . . . and Ozuma-san appeared!

Ozuma-san stood there, just as expressionless as ever. But this was the first time he had come to our café two days in a row. On top of that, he was carrying a large package on his back. After Ozuma-san confirmed my presence, he slid the package off his back and handed it to me.

"My apologies for yesterday. I was a bit too harsh."

Everything happened so quickly that I just stood there with my mouth open. Ozuma-san took my hand and urged me to open the package. Out came a huge Steiff Teddy Bear that was too big to wrap both arms around. Its big, black eyes stared right at me.

"Please keep up the good work. I hope you become a great maid," said Ozuma-san. Though he had a poker face, his feelings came through to me just fine. The next moment, all the Masters and maids inside the café applauded wildly. I was overcome with so much feeling that tears rolled down my cheeks. From that moment on, I vowed to be the best darn maid on Earth. And Major Lawrence, the Steiff Teddy Bear, became our café mascot.

Oh my God, how embarrassing. I haven't seen Ozuma-san since then, but Major Lawrence still sits in our break room. Even now, when I look into Major Lawrence's big, black eyes, I recall my earlier days as a rookie maid. This concludes my touching *polori* story!

November 30   A Master dropping by

This is my first entry. Aaliyah-chan, I always look forward to going to the café because you always greet me so cheerfully. But I noticed something strange. In your most recent essay, it's hard to say it without being blunt, but uhh . . . shouldn't it be "a touching *holori* story" rather than "a touching *polori* story" . . . ?

December 1   Aaliyah

Once upon a time, there was a Maid Kingdom. It was a legendary fairyland that existed somewhere on Earth. All of its citizens were maids. "Polori" was a term used in that country, meaning "immeasurable love."

During the Victorian era, a maid from the Maid Kingdom came to England. This maid not only protected her Master's large estate, but her service made possible the elegant balls he held every night. She became legendary for her peerless skill, and soon everyone knew the word "polori," which also denotes the maid's "service spirit."

Ever since that time, the best servant in the house has been called the Polori Master, and, at the beginning of each year is the Polori Fest, during which everyone puts on white brimmed headbands and chants "Poloooori! Poloori!" while dancing the polka. As he lay on his deathbed, Goethe's last words were the manly comment, "I want more *polori...*" Umm, er... I'll see you later! (Runs Away)

December 2   Yukino

Stop that crap. ^_^

December 3   Ruruka

You wrote ^_^ but your face isn't laughing. Oh, the horror . . . !

4

Even a Maiden's Strong Faith

Can Be Destroyed

Umm, regarding last week's essay, a Master pointed out my error. I meant to say "a touching *holori* story," not "a touching *polori* story." "*Polori*" sounds so . . . umm . . . perverted, doesn't it? Japanese is such a difficult language.

Umm, ahem. Well, what's done is done. Time to move on to today's essay!

Strange things happen when you work at a maid café.

After the three o'clock afternoon tea break, fewer Masters "came home" than usual, and things in the café settled down a bit. The maids were able to relax and do a little unwinding. During that time, a young Miss, about fourteen or fifteen years old, struggled to open the heavy door to "come home."

"Hi. Good afternoon . . ." she muttered.

"Welcome home, Miss Masami! ★"

I led her to a table and brought some milk tea. Miss Masami was a regular, so I knew exactly what she wanted. Usually, when I served her tea, Miss Masami smiled and said, "Thank you." But today, even when I served her favorite milk tea, Miss Masami didn't smile. Gosh, why is she so sad? Miss Masami never looked up. Instead, she stared down into her milk tea with a sad face. She didn't usually act like this. "Umm, Miss Masami, did something happen?"

Miss Masami mumbled, "I was hoping you could help me, Aaliyah-san. . . ."

It wasn't unusual to have customers seek advice at maid cafés. Many Masters and Misses in trouble have asked maids for help. As a maid, it's an honor to have Master or Miss rely on us. I wanted to say, "Miss Masami, I have your back! Troubles with love? Career plans? Makeup advice? No problem, I can help! I will gladly give you sound advice so that you may blossom in your beautiful youth! Lose the negative vibes, come to my safe haven, and pour your heart out to me!"

"Umm, I had a fight with my mother."

Oh, a very common problem indeed. It's quite natural for girls her age to clash with their parents. The problem can be resolved once you get to the heart of it. I just have to listen and carefully analyze the whole situation.

"We fought because Mother found a *doujinshi* in my room . . ."

Miss Masami drew *doujinshi*—self-published manga books—as a hobby. So much dedication at such a young age!

"Seems to me your mother was unreasonable to get angry over a *doujinshi*. Does your mother hate manga?"

"No. Actually, she loves manga."

I wondered how to tackle this. "You like to draw *doujin-*

shi, and your mother loves manga. There shouldn't be any problems, so what's wrong?"

Miss Masami shifted her eyes and fidgeted. Her hesitation indicated she wasn't quite ready to continue her story. After a long pause, her milk tea got cold, but Miss Masami finally spoke.

"It's a Boys Love (BL) *doujinshi.* . . ."

"Oh . . . hmm . . . that's yaoi (801) . . . about gays . . . a *doujinshi* about guys loving guys, right . . . ?"

My maid smile stiffened. I felt like a rookie soldier, frozen in place with my foot planted on the trigger switch of a land mine. Unfortunately, I didn't know how to respond to this sort of situation. I could have said, "There aren't any women who hates gays," but of course, there are some girls who don't particularly care for gays, so I'd be lying. The gap between gay-loving girls and gay-ignorant girls was as deep as the Mariana Trench.

But despite my helplessness, Miss Masami continued to explain her predicament.

"Mother yelled at me and said, 'Stop drawing sleazy manga!' I . . . I don't know what to do."

Long, long ago, while I sat in my father's lap, he told me, "Aaliyah, you need to be extremely careful when dealing with BL manga. The girls who love BL have so much passion for it, that passion will suck them in and destroy everything in sight, like a powerful Megiddo Flame." Of course, my father never said that (it was a joke!), but nevertheless, you need to be cautious when discussing the world of gay love. In my opinion, *wabi-sabi* and gay love top the list of touchy, delicate, and complicated subjects. Gay love discussions are often charged with emotion. One slip of the tongue and you could get dragged into a vicious debate of who is the *uke* and who is the *seme*. The best way to describe *uke* and *seme* is . . . er . . . umm . . . with gay couples, *uke* is the "feminine role" and *seme* is the "masculine role," I guess. They also write it as "A × B." A is the *seme* and B is the *uke*. It's also called a "coupling." Girls who love BL have endless debates on which characters are *uke* and which *seme*. Differences in coupling opinions sometimes result in breakups of friendships. Oh my gosh . . . why am I giving a lecture on this stuff via the Internet to the whole world . . . ?

"I'm sorry. I troubled you, didn't I?"

After seeing my puzzled expression, Miss Masami forced herself to smile. I didn't know what to say. I hung my head in shame and could only watch Miss Masami leave the café.

My reputation as a trustworthy and dependable maid was shot all to hell.

I felt useless. I couldn't lift Miss Masami's spirits. A maid who's supposed to give comfort to her customers couldn't even solve one young girl's problem. I wasn't qualified to be a maid. I'm a total disgrace to maids. How can I call myself a maid if I can't even solve one little gay problem or two?

I was determined to solve this problem one way or another, so I ran to Yukino-san during her break and explained the situation. "Please teach me everything you know about gays so I can save Miss Masami!"

Yukino-san looked straight into my eyes and asked, "Before I do that, why me?"

"When I thought of gays, I thought of you!"

I knew that Yukino-san is the most knowledgeable person about gay stuff in this café. She'll always assume that two male characters in any story are not friends, but lovers. She'll read normal manga anthologies, like *Shonen Jump,* and somehow twist them into sordid gay love stories. On her days off, she'll buy piles of BL manga at shops at Ikebukuro's Otome Road.

"Please teach me the way of yaoi appreciation!"

"Hmm . . ." Yukino-san rubbed her chin and pondered for a while. Then she suddenly grabbed my neck, Spock-style, and dragged me into the locker room. Yukino-san rifled through her locker and dumped a pile of manga with men doing kinky things with each other!

"Fine. If you want to learn about it so badly, I'll teach you . . . EVERYTHING."

Yukino-san's eyes sparkled mysteriously. Had I finally pressed Yukino-san's buttons? The usually calm and collected Yukino-san was now fiery hot with passion. Oh gosh, I'd totally pushed her "gay love" button. "I only want to learn enough to help Miss Masami out, not enter the world of yaoi! So . . . please . . . gosh . . . oh . . . wow . . ."

It was a world unlike anything I'd ever experienced before in my life.

Yukino-san went into an unexplored area of my brain and pioneered a new way of thinking. She taught me the concepts of an inviting *uke,* a goofy *uke,* and an all-aggressive *seme.* Personally, I preferred the type of character who seemed overbearing on the surface, but actually cared about his lover in subtle ways. Like when the character saw his crush flirting with another guy . . . the character would run to the back of the gym, flustered. It's so adorable. Also, the all-aggressive *seme* with a vulnerable side really gripped my heart. . . .

Wait! I must focus on my original mission. I need to help Miss Masami out of her funk. I'm fine. I am no longer ignorant on gay subjects. I, Aaliyah Kominami (with enhanced yaoi appreciation skills), will save the day! It's time for a second round of gay love problem-solving. I e-mailed Miss Masami to have her come back to the café. I had to do it while I was still roaring with BL passion!

"Yes, Aaliyah-san . . . ?"

Miss Masami seemed a bit confused, since she was called out by a maid who couldn't help her the first time around. Her troubled look reaffirmed my determination to help this troubled teenaged girl. My pride as a maid was on the line. This time, I would provide sound advice to guide her on the right path of life!

"So, Miss Masami, your mother doesn't object to you drawing manga, correct?"

"That's correct. Mother insisted that there are other types of manga I could draw that would make a real contribution to society. She said I could read and draw those types of manga."

"So your mother feels yaoi is filthy and immoral, right? She's so close, yet so far. I appreciate the fact that she considers manga to be a valuable cultural asset, but I wish she'd also acknowledge and appreciate the world of yaoi."

"But no matter what I said, Mother wasn't convinced. . . ."

Miss Masami sadly looked down, and I said, "But don't worry! I figured out the ultimate solution to this deceptively difficult problem, so you can continue drawing *and* make up with your mother. If you follow my directions, your mother will surely approve. The solution is . . ."

"The solution is . . . ?"

"Miss Masami, you need to draw the world's best gay love manga!"

"Huh?"

"Your gay love manga will have to be so good it will slowly brainwash your mother. Do or die. You need to draw a gay love manga that will give your mother a total change of heart. Pour your soul into a spectacular BL manga that your mother would want to recommend to her friends. A story that surpasses the mainstream classics! Miss Masami, you must draw manga that will someday revolutionize your mother!"

Miss Masami was taken aback by my powerful advice, but when she came to, she replied, "Yes! I need to draw a manga that Mother will love!"

"Absolutely! Great manga is not based on whether it's yaoi or not. Dream big! Miss Masami, you will be the greatest yaoi manga artist ever. A master of yaoi. You'll sell a billion yaoi manga books. Your yaoi stories will be adapted into movies shown all over the world, and win Academy Awards as the first yaoi movie based on yaoi manga!"

I held hands with Miss Masami and we shared our passion

for yaoi. Miss Masami was so fired up that she darted out of the café, itching to draw her best yaoi manga ever. Her eyes were filled with hope and fiery passion. Miss Masami, I look forward to reading the world's best yaoi manga—drawn by you!

Thus, a maid helped a troubled Mistress again today. If you have any problems or concerns, go ask a maid for help. We look forward to solving your problems! ★

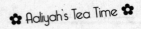

✿ Aaliyah's Tea Time ✿

A message board connecting maids
and Masters! ✿ Please send us your comments!

December 5   Snow White

The world of gay love manga seems so complicated. Can you please teach a newbie about it? What does "Otome Road," "inviting _uke_," and "all-aggressive _seme_" mean? ^_^ Also, what did Yukino-san teach you in her "Yaoi 101" class?

December 6   Aaliyah

I'm just a novice in the gay love manga world, too, but I will try to best answer your question, Miss Snow White.

I mentioned it in my essay already, but gay love manga, called "yaoi (801)" or "Boys Love" (BL), are stories where gay guys love other gay guys. Ninety-nine percent of these books are bought by women (which is why it's also considered "comics for women"). In many _otaku_ shops, there is a section dedicated to yaoi.

Otome Road is a 200-meter strip of road out of the Ikebukuro East Exit, in front of the Sunshine 60 skyscraper. It has a lot of stores targeting female manga readers. "Inviting _uke_" and "all-aggressive _seme_" are... umm... if I define them here, then the images of "wholesome maids" won't be so "wholesome" anymore.... I hope you can allow me to refrain from answering that question, or else the organization starting with the letter P, with the middle letter T, and the last letter A will hunt me down like a witch, take me to a religious court, and burn these books at the stake. Please forgive me.... [FX] TREMBLE TREMBLE

Oh, in Yukino-san's class, I got locked up in the room for three days straight, where she forced to me to read yaoi manga and novels. While I slept, Yukino-san whispered BL novels into my ear. After cramming so many gay love stories into my head, I no longer cried, or laughed, or...

December 6   Yukino

It was just a plain old lecture, thank you. ^_^

December 7   Ruruka

You're not really smiling (again) ...!

5

So, You Want to Work

at a Maid Café?

Question: What's the most important thing at a maid café?

The maids, of course. If you take the maids from a maid café, it would just be a café. False-advertising complaints would be lodged to JARO for the maid café sign.

Then what makes a maid a *maid*? I'm sure some of you out there answered, "Maid outfits!"—from the orthodox black or dark blue maid outfits worn by homely women to colorful pastel-colored maid outfits with frills and ribbons. Of course, paying attention to details, such as one's outfit, is quite important, but there's something even more essential to being a great maid than that.

Here's the answer. . . .

The most important thing about being a maid is *the proper maid mind-set*!

Think about it. Take, for example, the simple service of drawing a picture on *omu-rice* with ketchup. How would the Master feel if a lifeless, droopy maid drew the picture with a lazy, bored attitude? How would a Master feel about a muscular guy, over six feet tall, wearing a tight maid out-fit ripping at the seams, gleefully announcing, "Let me draw a cute picture for you! ★" Horrible! Let me repeat. Horrible! The most important part of maid service is anticipating your Master's needs and then giving him the most appropriate service and care. Without that mind-set, a maid café would transform into an ordinary café staffed by people in maid costumes.

After closing time, I helped with the cleanup and waved goodbye to my coworkers as they left. I brought a stack of resumes over to my laptop. I've been doing this extra-duty after-hours work for the past few days, so I was pretty sleepy. But I wanted to help find the best new maid for our café.

Last month, one of our maids quit. We wished her luck as she moved on, but until we found a new person, everyone had to work at a hectic pace to cover the loss. The café was insanely busy and the work exceeded our capacity, so all of us complained to Makoto-tencho. She finally gave in and said, "Let's hire a new employee."

Makoto-tencho announced the job opening in several ads, and lo and behold, a whole bunch of applicants sent in their resumes. I was surprised to see so many applicants interested in our tiny little café. Makoto-tencho hugged a large pile of resumes and asked, "Aaliyah-chan, can you help me choose a few candidates? Let's split it up. Here, take this half."

Though I had no idea why she tasked me with this project, I agreed to assist her in the selection process. I stared at the resumes so hard that I could have blazed holes in them. I reviewed each resume several times over, analyzed the contents, and entered the assessment data into my laptop. For some reason, Makoto-tencho's share was considerably smaller than my share . . . but, oh well, I decided, I'll do my best, because once the new maid is hired, I'll have a junior employee below me and won't be the low man on the totem pole anymore! As Akihabara's famous maid trainer (*joke!*), I'll use my keen eyes to uncover real maid talent. I'll find a diamond in the rough. I'll discover a budding maid, aiming to be the world's best, just like me!

For those of you interested in working at a maid café, let me explain the general selection procedures. First, the café will sort through the resumes to select a group of viable candidates for interviews. The competition to be a maid is a lot tougher these days, and the café owners are so busy actually running their cafés they don't have time to interview every single applicant. That's why the first phase of the selection process is simply screening the resumes. I swear, we are not making paper airplanes out of the resumes and selecting the farthest-flying one . . . or burning the resumes to find the fastest-burning one . . . or using a Ouija board to choose our maids! We are doing this in a serious manner (though I guess some other cafés might just choose their maids randomly). I urged Ruruka-san to get serious about the selection, I won't let her ruin my chances of finding a great new junior employee!

Each resume is filled with that person's hopes and dreams, so it's extremely heart-wrenching to restrict the number of applicants that make it to the next stage. But . . . some resumes are . . . somewhat questionable. Working at a maid café is just like any other job. Putting in silly photos of your face from a print club is bad. You shouldn't fill out the form with a sparkly pen. Don't use cutesy but illegible fonts, either. And please write in Japanese. We can barely make out English, but Latin, Swahili, and archaic languages are cryptic at best, and those resumes will definitely end up in the shredder. Also, what is up with guys applying for maid jobs? Why do they put heinous photos of themselves in maid outfits on their resumes? They need to kneel on a stone with Ruruka-san and think real deep and hard about why their mothers gave birth to them in the first place!

Cough, cough. Excuse me, I'm a little snappy because I haven't had much sleep. Let me continue with the resume screening. Hmm? This person listed her objectives in bullet form. I guess it's okay, format-wise. Well, let's see . . . the reason she applied is . . .

- Maid outfits are cute
- I want to be a maid
- I hear the job is easy
- Everybody's doing it these days!
- ★ I want a very easy job, please ★

Disqualified. Dropped. Rejected. Reeeally, think about it. Maids must provide timely, caring service. If you write a resume without thinking about the employers who'll read it, how can you think about your Master's needs? A maid must instantly determine what's best for her Master, based on his speech and mannerisms, and provide the most appropriate service. One must learn to deduce from his behavior a Master's personality, hobbies and preferences, needs, et cetera. A maid must adapt her speech patterns and behavior to satisfy each Master. Sensitivity is the key for maids!

Excuse me . . . I'm cranky, aren't I? I'll have some tea to calm myself down, and review the resumes that passed the screening. Oh wow, these future hopefuls shine with potential. Those who write resumes properly will surely be proper maids as well. . . . Hmm? I noticed my own corrections on the margin of this resume. I missed it when I sorted through this pile. Let's see . . .

"I wrote a song! Please use this as a theme song for your café! Please see the back. ⇨"

Huh . . . ? A song . . . ?

♫ MAID MARCH ♫

See Akihabara's blue sky!
Inhale the rich aroma of Darjeeling tea!
Can you hear the steps of the laced-up boots?
The immaculately proper, the unwavering . . .
Ahh maids, oh maids, ahh maids.

See the maid café's pink sky
Their aprons and dresses sparkle every day
Can you hear them say, "Welcome home, Master"?
The absolute territory, unwavering
Ahh maids, oh maids, ahh maids. (*)
(* refrain)

P-Please go away . . . !

I tossed the maid song resume into the reject pile and slumped my shoulders in disgust. With dark clouds forming over my head, I really couldn't see the whole point of this resume. As a maid, I was used to comforting others, but I needed some comforting myself after reading that trash. Can someone please shoot me up with a tranquilizer to ease my pain? I'm really glad that this person applied, but I believe her efforts went in a totally wrong direction. I wonder if I'll ever find a really good junior maid.

Several days later, we were able to narrow down the pool of candidates to just a handful. Let's go to the next phase of the selection process . . . the interviews!

After closing time, Makoto-tencho and I sat next to each other, waiting for the candidates. We had to interview each person carefully and determine her potential as a maid. We could choose only one person, so no mistakes were allowed.

The first person entered. The girl was a little late for her appointed time slot, but she was wearing a frilly maid outfit, jumped into the room, and squealed in a high-pitched voice, "Gooood evening! Nice to meeeet you!"

She didn't show an ounce of guilt for being late. Oh gosh, we had started off with a problem child . . . cough, cough. You didn't hear that. Just because you're applying for a job at a maid café doesn't mean that you come to an interview in a maid outfit. Maid outfits are just "uniforms" for the job, so you don't really wear it all the time. Makoto-tencho and I were wearing regular clothes. If you went to a job interview wearing your swimsuit for a race queen spot, the employers wouldn't know what to do with you. Makoto-tencho explained in a roundabout way that she didn't need to wear a maid outfit to this interview.

But the girl pouted her lips and retorted, "Whaaat!! Did I do something wrooooong?"

Uhh, I really wish there was a button under the table that would have opened a trapdoor underneath the girl and dropped her out of sight. We really needed that button! If we didn't have one, we needed to make one ASAP! It would be awesome if we filled the bottom of the hole with sticky mud or flour, too.

My face almost twitched, but Makoto-tencho kept her cool. Her smile was permanently planted on her face. No wonder she's the manager, and not me, hmm! Makoto-tencho pushed up her glasses twice. Before the interview, we'd come up with a secret sign. If either of us pushed up our glasses two times in a row, the candidate was an immediate failure!

"Okay. Thank you very much. We'll send our results of this interview later."

"Okey-dokey! Thank you soooo much! ★"

"Yes, take care."

Makoto-tencho gave curt replies to the girl's remarks and cut off the fifteen-minute interview in five minutes. The silly girl pranced out of the room, humming a happy song, completely unaware of her nonselection. Makoto-tencho maintained her smile throughout the entire painful interview. She never lost her cool. Actually, she seemed more cold and cruel than cool. Brr . . .

A maid job is just like any other part-time job. Generally,

we'll go over questions such as the candidate's reason for applying, hours available, and commuting distance. We'll ask specific questions pertaining to maid cafés too, asking if they have any negative feelings toward *otaku*s or how their families feel about their employment as a maid and such. Even if they aren't into *otaku* culture much, they get bonus points for liking a specific anime or game or two. Finally, a maid candidate has to have some sort of adorable look or quality. There are only certain sizes of maid outfits, so they must be able to fit in size 9 or smaller. This was one of the tougher standards to meet. Oh, we mentioned that maid outfits weren't recommended for interviews but that cute clothes were highly welcomed and Gothic and Lolita type clothes were fine.

If you want to become a maid, please consider all the advice I just gave you as precious words from heaven and chant them three times!

Oh, then the next applicant arrived. She came on time and spoke properly. She might be a good candidate, we figured.

"I made a maid song! Please listen!"

Makoto-tencho quietly pushed up her glasses twice.

After going through a number of hopeless war casualties, we were almost finished with the interviews. Makoto-tencho and I hadn't been able to find a viable candidate among those interviewed thus far. We were down to our last interviewee. Let's see, this was a resume that passed Makoto-tencho's screening. But, umm, this person was . . .

"Good evening. Nice to meet you."

A male entered.

6

The Maid Café Waiter

It's been a week since Kiriya-san, the waiter, began work at our café.

"I may require some assistance until I get used to this job. Thank you." Kiriya-san, a tall gentleman, bowed and introduced himself properly. But he was so perfect. He never needed any help from us.

Both Makoto-tencho and I gave him perfect marks during his interview the other day. Compared to the other disasters we interviewed, he gave solid responses, had many employable skills, and had a good mind-set and attitude. After the string of hopeless interviews, he shined through like a ray of light from heaven. But Makoto-tencho admitted that we were taking a chance in hiring a male waiter instead of a maid.

We hired Kiriya-san as a waiter and chef, freeing Makoto-tencho to leave the kitchen and work in the main hall. As a result, it increased the number of maids in the café. But first, we had to ensure the food would be of the same quality. Of course, maid cafés hardly require a four-star restaurant chef to prepare their meals, but nonetheless, they still need someone with basic cooking skills. Maybe a few Masters might feel cheated being served dishes prepared by a male chef instead of a cute maid, but . . . we don't mean to deceive anyone! To tell you the truth, most maid cafés have male chefs cooking meals. I'm sure Masters often wonder if a "Maid's Creamy Beef Stew" was really made by a maid, but in reality, it's usually made by a beefy man in sweats, dishing out his stew with a grunt. But we're not lying, exaggerating, or cheating anyone. Umm . . . er . . . uhh . . . I promise, all of the meals served at our maid café are made with maid magic. Ruruka-san's magical European skills put spells on the dishes. So please don't lodge any complaints to JARO's customer service hotline! Shudder, shudder . . .

Sorry for getting off track. Kiriya-san had amazing cooking skills. By the end of his first day, he had mastered all the menu dishes. Makoto-tencho was so impressed by his skills that her jaw dropped open and her glasses almost fell off. He sliced lemons in a blur, and whipped cream at the speed of sound.

"Have you worked as a chef before?"

"Yes, a little," said Kiriya-san, giving us a megawatt teen-idol smile. On top of that, this multitalented gentleman helped wait tables when the café got busy and raised the efficiency of the café. The Mistresses started whispering about this rare male character in Akihabara. Come to think of it, more Mistresses have been "coming home" to our café these days.

So obviously, Kiriya-san was fitting in without any problems.

But there was one thing I was worried about.

- - -

The other day, I went with Kiriya-san to buy some Christmas decorations and lighting for our café. Maid cafés usually have cheerful Christmas decorations, in the spirit of the season. I was assigned to buy the decorations this year.

"I know a good shop. Shall we go there?" suggested Kiriya-san.

Kiriya-san volunteered to shop with me. We took a midshift break to shop at a store he recommended. We bought blue Christmas lights, Santa and reindeer candles, Christmas wreaths, and a Santa outfit.

On the way back, we held large bags in both arms as we waited on the platform for the train. We'd shopped at a cheap store, so we might have bought too much stuff. I carried a fairly large bag, but Kiriya-san had a bag three times bigger than mine over his shoulder. "A-Are you okay?"

"I'm fine," he said, smiling. The train finally arrived, and we got on, Kiriya-san carrying his huge bag with ease.

"There aren't too many people riding trains at this time of day, huh?"

We set our bags on the floor and took a breather. The train was generally empty during the day, so we had a lot of space to ourselves. If we were caught in a rush, it wouldn't have been pretty, though.

But . . .

SHAKA-LAKA-SHAKA-LAKA-SHAKA-LAKA . . .

A guy with huge headphones was listening to his music way too loud. He closed his eyes and rhythmically rocked his head to the song. He obviously had no manners. His music was so loud that we could clearly hear the singer's voice. Oh gosh . . . he was listening to the theme song of the video game Miko Miko Nurse. The song itself was upbeat and all, but loudly blasting an adults-only pervert game song in a public place is a mild form of a terrorist attack. Just because he was approaching Akihabara didn't mean he could disturb others. He was ignoring manners and morals like an armored vehicle viciously running over innocent people. We needed the FBI to drag him out by the shoulders and lock him up or something.

But in a typical Japanese fashion, everyone on the train tried their best to ignore the idiot's loud music. A grandmother's face was getting pale, a mother with a young child wanted to move to a different car, and high school girls were trembling in fear, but all of them tried to tolerate the situation as best they could. Even if the nurse character dressed as a temple priestess *was* trying to hold back her feelings toward her crush in this bittersweet love song, everyone in the train was trying really hard not to hear it. That's why I was also just enduring the pain. Kiriya-san was also . . . huh?

Suddenly Kiriya-san, with his trademark smile, pulled out a 10,000-yen bill—roughly $100—from his wallet and folded it in half twice. What was he trying to do? Ah . . . oh gosh . . . he put the folded bill into the headphone guy's breast pocket!

"You're too loud," Kiriya-san complained, as he pulled out a pair of scissors from his pocket. He snipped the headphone cord!

U-Umm . . .

Everyone on the train, including the headphone guy and me, just stood there with our mouths gaping open, without fully understanding what just happened. The loud music gave off a static sound, followed by dead silence. Kiriya-san tucked his wallet and scissors back into his pocket and faced the window, looking at the moving scenery as if nothing had happened.

"Hey . . . wait!" the headphone guy growled at Kiriya-san. But Kiriya-san wasn't intimidated at all. He just stared down at the headphone guy.

"Urkk . . ." the headphone guy swallowed, powerless against the force of Kiriya-san's glare. After they'd locked eyes for a while, the (former) headphone guy clicked his tongue and fled to the next car. Kiriya-san turned back to the window and looked out.

The people remaining in the train stared in disbelief at Kiriya-san. Of course, I'm sure they appreciated that he'd put a stop to the offensive music, but his actions had them frozen in fear.

"Aaliyah-san."

Y-Yes!

"I . . . want to change . . . the café."

I really didn't know how to respond to his sudden comment. But Kiriya-san continued.

"Our café isn't perfect. I'm not satisfied with our staffing procedures and the way events are held. We're not professional enough. Unless the café improves in those areas, it'll never become a great café."

Kiriya-san shared his opinions about the café as he stood

there, staring at the outside scenery. I wanted to say, "Let's work together to make a great café then!" but after witnessing such a shocking event, all I could do was nod in acknowledgment.

Before I could say anything, the train arrived in Akihabara.

Once we returned to the café, we began to decorate inside. We placed candles and little Christmas trees on each table, and hung colorful Christmas lighting on the walls. We had so many ornaments and strings of light that we decorated everything in sight. The dreamy, fantasy-filled garbage can . . . an electrical parade toilet brush . . . we went overboard, but oh well, it was all in the name of fun!

I noticed a crowd of maids around Kiriya-san in the break room. What was going on?

"Kiriya-san suggested that we make a *doujinshi* for our café."

The maids were discussing what type of *doujinshi* to draw. It was a new concept for the maids in this café, so they seemed pretty excited by the radical idea. Kiriya-san had already calculated estimated costs, number of pages, and recommended publishers. He was as quick a thinker as he was a cook.

"I want to change the café for the better, and everyone in the café should feel so, too."

I remembered Kiriya-san's comment as he got off the train. I wondered how Kiriya-san's ideas would change our café.

7

The Maids Go to Comiket

There are many types of festivals in this world.

Half-naked dancers at the Carnival in Rio de Janeiro . . . people throwing tomatoes at one another in Spain's La Tomatina . . . people dressed as cats at Belgium's Cat Parade—there are an infinite number of bizarre festivals around the world. People seek relief from life's miseries at these festivals. They revive the spirit.

In Japan, our festival is the Comic Market, or Comiket.

This event boasts the largest number of *doujinshi* sold in Japan . . . no, the world. It's held in one of the world's largest convention halls, Tokyo Big Sight. At Comiket, both amateur and professional artists make appearances, buying and selling *doujinshi*. It isn't just a small gathering of wannabe artists showcasing their handmade zines. There are more than 400,000 attendees annually, or the equivalent of the whole population of Brunei (including babies and senior citizens). Because of the festival's large size and history, many legends and rumors have been born, such as . . . the collective heat and passion from the enthusiastic participants deflected a typhoon . . . or attracted storm clouds . . . or the son of a particular northern country's president showed up . . . or the esteemed Royal Couple attended with their newborn baby, among other popular rumors and legends.

We were approaching the time for another Comiket! Actually . . . this was the first time, I, Aaliyah Kominami, had ever attended a Comiket. The busiest times of the year for maid cafés were during this festival. Comiket is held twice a year, once during the summer, and once at the end of the year. Also, a lot of *otaku*s from all over Japan migrate to Tokyo just to attend Comiket. Twice a year, it doubles the number of *otaku*s in Tokyo, causing a massive concentration of *otaku* power. Naturally, the *otaku*s would generally attend the Comiket first, and then visit maid cafés afterward. It was popular to have fun at the Comiket during the day, then party in maid cafés at night. During Comiket, the pace of life in a maid café is completely different from the rest of the year. An unbelievable number of Masters and Mistresses "come home." Of course, this means the maids have to shift into turbo mode to serve everyone. I've always wanted to go to a Comiket, but because of the café's busy rush, I never had a chance until now.

Because after Kiriya-san came to work at our café, the situation drastically changed.

"It turns out that one of the *doujinshi* clubs couldn't man their booth, so they offered it to us," Kiriya-san explained. "Let's make a photo book of our maids. That way, we don't have to create a manga from scratch. I'll be glad to shoot some photos, and edit them, too. We can extend the deadline a bit. I've already made arrangements with a publisher."

Kiriya-san had suggested that our café make a *doujin-shi*. Usually, in order to acquire a selling booth at the Comiket (a super-rare opportunity!), a group has to fill out an application six months ahead and get selected by lottery . . . under very harsh odds. But at the last minute, Kiriya-san was able to borrow a space from a group that couldn't use it. On top of that, Kiriya-san took pictures of maids, used graphics software to organize the photos, and sent the order to the publishers at a good pace. Before we knew it, we'd set up everything way before the Comiket began.

Of course, the maids rushed up and down the stairs to help with the preparations for the event. We ran around like headless chickens, trying to work on a project that we'd never done before. The finished books were shipped to Kiriya-san. Kiriya-san, Ruruka-san, and I were on the first day's shift to sell the books.

The first day of Comiket!

Ruruka-san and I were on the Rinkai Line and got off at the Kokusai Tenjijo Station. Like African Maasai tribal warriors seeing modern civilization for the first time, Ruruka-san and I were awed at the sight.

It was 6:30 A.M. Cold sea breezes blew over the sidewalks from the coast. The sidewalks were just *filled* with people. The sun wasn't up yet, but the place was jam-packed, so much so that even a little kitty couldn't squeeze in. The massive line led to the large triangular silhouette of the Tokyo Big Sight hall. It would usually take only ten minutes to walk to it from the station, but today it felt like the passage to India.

"Are we still in Japan . . . ?" asked Ruruka-san.

Ruruka-san, who usually played the "quirky character" in the café, was also a Comiket virgin like me, and didn't have the luxury to act out her character. She just stood with her mouth agape. I was pulling a heavy cart full of our freshly printed books, but had the same reaction as her. We had totally underestimated Comiket.

I recalled Yukino-san's pep talk: "Drink a vitamin drink and get through it with some pizzazz."

Each day of Comiket is divided up among different genres. For example, the first day of the Winter Comiket was *doujinshi* aimed toward female fans, and the second day was geared toward male fans. In somewhat blunt un-PC terms, the first day was gay love stuff, and the second day was perverted stuff. Yukino-san, a Crusader for the Yaoi Kingdom, attended the first day of Comiket as a buyer. Last night, after a whole day of battle in the Yaoi Kingdom, Yukino-san and I met briefly at the café during the shift changeover. She looked beat. I wanted to add the subtitle "I'm burned out (from all the gay manga) . . ." on her back. Back in the break room, Yukino-san was no longer the older-sister figure who had so cheerfully advised us to "drink some vitamin drinks and get through it with pizzazz," but instead just another crazed yaoi fan, chuckling with delight as she flipped through pages of her war trophies (yaoi *doujinshi*). She usually kept her guilty pleasures to herself, but this time she was openly displaying her enjoyment.

I never took Comiket seriously, even after seeing Yukino-san with the life drained out of her, but it turned out I was the most naïve little toilet beetle ever. But . . . I couldn't run away now. "Retreat" is not an option for Aaliyah Kominami. I had to do better than the exhausted Yukino-san. I clenched my fists, gritted my teeth, and decided to jump into the massive line. "Ruruka-san, hold my hand so we can survive this battle!"

". . . Hmm? Ruruka-san?" I asked.

Ruruka-san announced, "After this event is over . . . I'm returning to my hometown to marry. I'll leave the underworld and move on," as she handed her cart handle to me. "Aaliyah-chan, think of these books as me, and take care of it, okay? Leave the rest to me, and move forward. Look ahead! The goal is right in front of you! Go! And don't look back!"

Ruruka-san twirled around and tried to jump back onto the train we'd just gotten off of. I grabbed the back of her collar, though. *Tsk*. You can't fool me by spouting cliché phrases of farewell from anime.

"Lucifer's curse will torment you to death!" she warned.

Ignoring Ruruka-san's empty threats, I grabbed her right hand, leaned forward, pulled the heavy cart with my left hand, and squatted at the end of the huge line. With strong determination, I entered the Comiket.

We were in line for only thirty minutes, but it felt like an eternity. It was extremely cold. I'm not sure if it was because the Ariake port was made from landfill, but the chilly winds blew across it mercilessly. On top of that, we were forced to stand still in that crowded line and couldn't budge an inch in any direction. They crammed us in like this because they were expecting ten thousand or more exhibitors. But they packed us in too tight. Prisoners in Siberia and tribal slaves in Africa were given a little more space than this. If someone dared to leave a small gap in the line, one of the staffers would yell out, "Hey, over there! There are a few inches of open space! Close it up!"

"But if we close it up any more, our bones will be crushed like a compressed metal chunk in a scrap metal factory! Even POWs get better treatment. Did you know that POWs are protected under the Geneva Convention . . . ?"

"Hurry up! Close it up!"

"Geneva . . . umm . . . uhh . . ."

"Now!"

I'm sorry. It's all my fault. I'll fold my body in a little tighter. "Sorry, sorry, sorry . . ."

What would be my cause of death? Hypothermia? Or being crushed to death? All the other participants were squatting, unable to move as well, and enduring the cold. Oh, I wondered, What is Kiriya-san doing? We're supposed to meet at the booth, so he must be somewhere in this line. I'll give him a call. Umm, Kiriya-san's number is . . .

"—unable to reach at this time. Please call back. . . ."

Hmm, that's funny. My cell phone worked fine, so why was I getting this funny message? It wasn't a busy signal, either. How strange. I asked Ruruka-san to call him with her cell.

"Unable to reach at this time. Please call back...."

Ruruka-san got the same message. W-Wait. Was this the rumored "Comiket dead cell phone" situation, where so many people at the Comiket used their cell phones at once, it caused the signals to cancel out and the cell phones turned into worthless plastic junk?

"Please call back later.... Please call back later...."

I couldn't wait!

Argh...! I was getting irritated. A phrase crossed my mind... "common sense and absurdities specific to the Comiket." I really didn't think this place was filled with dreams, fantasies, and fairy tales (the bad kind). If we used the Comiket vendor tickets Kiriya-san gave us, I figured we should be able to enter the convention center without any problems. We had to endure this just a little longer. We didn't know when and where we needed to show the vendor tickets, but we could only trust Kiriya-san's words for now!

7:10 a.m.

No movement in line. It's cold.

7:20 a.m.

My teeth are about to fall out from the biting cold. Ruruka-san is spouting evil curses every five seconds. She's scaring the crap out of me.

7:34 a.m.

Ruruka-san tried to curse everyone with her black magic. A staff member stopped her in under seven seconds.

8:10 a.m.

I wanted to go to the bathroom, but there was a long line

for that, too. I wanted to cry when the staffer announced, "The end of the bathroom line is over theeeeeere."

8:45 a.m.

It was 3 degrees Celsius. Cold, moderate winds from the north. Ice was forming on Ruruka-san.

9:11 a.m.

I clutched my vendor tickets and gritted my teeth. Once we showed the tickets, we'd be saved. But we didn't know how or when to use them. Oh gosh. Ruruka-san hadn't moved in a long time.

9:22 a.m.

My knees and back are crying in pain. I'd sell my soul for some warm air and a hot cup of tea right now.

9:34 a.m.

I'm too afraid to confirm whether Ruruka-san has stopped breathing or not.

9:45 a.m.

My fingers shook so hard that I couldn't doodle in my memo pad. Oh gosh, Ruruka-san was finally . . . oh . . . no . . .

. . . By the time Ruruka-san and I entered the convention center, we looked like death frozen over. We looked like Yukino-san did yesterday. We never found out when to use the vendor tickets. But there was no time to waste now. The festival had already begun. Oh my gosh. We needed to set up our booth, pronto. Otherwise, our vacant booth would look empty and lonely. We weren't allowed to run inside the hall, so we speed-walked through the hallway.

We walked like walkathon athletes as we beelined to our booth.

"You guys are late," Kiriya-san said at the booth, already prepped and ready to go. The immaculate ad board was propped up, and the books were in neat piles. He even seemed relaxed, sitting there sipping his cup of tea.

"Kiriya-san, what time did you arrive to beat the crowd out there?" I asked.

"I wasn't that early. I arrived at the station around 8:30 A.M."

He came later than us!

"If you used the vendor tickets, you could have entered easily. Didn't you use them?"

"But we didn't know when or where to use them! We lined up at the station and waited all this time! That's why we're late!" I exclaimed.

"The vendor line and the general admission line are different. If you lined up in the general admission line, then of course you'd be late. Oh, did I not tell you about the different lines?" Kiriya-san asked, as he gulped down the hot cup of tea.

. . . Ruruka-san, please use black magic, temple curses, voodoo dolls, or whatever. . . . Please curse Kiriya-san and make him go to hell. . . .

8

Maid Passes Out at Comiket!

The Comiket attendees looked so cheerful.

Countless numbers of colorful *doujinshi* titles were piled on long rows of tables in the huge hall. Many participants carried backpacks, a few club members pulled carts full of their *doujinshi,* and a bunch of glamorous cosplayers were strutting around. They were all too busy braving the cold to enjoy themselves at the festival.

Amid the excitement, I curled up in my cheap folding chair and tried to stay warm in the frigid convention hall.

Shiver shiver shiver . . . My teeth chattered so much that my jaw almost fell off. It felt like I was being forced into a military death march through snow. Our booth was right next to the entrance, so every time a wave of people poured into the hall, the chilly northerly winds blew in with them. I thought I was going to catch a bad cold at any minute. Squatting down in the shape of a Tetris-z block and enduring the frozen oceanic wind for more than three hours was just too much for me. I'll probably turn into a frozen maid Popsicle, I thought. I might turn into another Comiket legend—the maid who tried to endure the cold Comiket winds, but ended her short life as a faithful dog (no, as Aaliyah, the faithful maid) awaiting her Master. Everyone at Comiket will mourn me, and the day will be designated as a national holiday called "Maid Day" in honor of my death. Every year on Maid Day, young men and women will face Akihabara to observe a period of silence for thirty minutes, and a bronze statue of a maid will be erected in front of Tokyo Big Sight. The maid statue will become a popular landmark used for a couple's meeting place. . . .

"Aaliyah-san, are you okay?"

Hah!

Kiriya-san called me back to Earth. Oh gosh, this was really bad. I was feeling a bit feverish, and was drifting in and out of consciousness. But I couldn't pass out here. Ruruka-san had gone home, so Kiriya-san and I were the only ones left to sell the *doujinshi*.

"Now that the Northern Stars have reached nirvana, I must channel my chakra when I return to the divine position," Ruruka-san had said.

A rough translation of this gibberish: She's cold, sleepy, and tired, so she's going home.

"Ruruka-san, you just got here. It's too early to leave!" I wanted to say to her, but after seeing her face, half-frozen and blue like a wax doll, I didn't have the heart to stop her from leaving. I was barely alive, but in better condition than Ruruka-san, so I'd hold the fort with my life!

"This is the coin box, and here are the bills. Aaliyah-san, you hand them the books."

Kiriya-san was amazing as usual. By the time we arrived

(late), he had already set up the booth and was ready to go. I'd struggled to drag the heavy load of books, but Kiriya-san had brought all the other necessary business items, such as a tablecloth, coin box, and money bag. In addition, he had made a pop-up display full of maid photos so our booth could stand out from the others.

"Umm . . . don't we have too many books?" I asked Kiriya-san.

We had about two hundred maid photo books. Wasn't that a few too many for a new group jumping in at the last minute? I'd heard the world of *doujinshi* was very tough. The number of copies sold ranged from a handful to several thousand, creating a hierarchy among the groups. Many groups have attempted to climb to the top of the formidable *doujinshi* ladder, but in vain.

"But we're here to sell books, aren't we?" Kiriya-san asked back. Hmm, bold words indeed.

"Oh yes, I haven't seen the finished copy of the book yet. Let me see. Oh, uh-huh, hmm, really . . ." The photos of all the maids were adorable and unique. The background colors and designs matched each maid's qualities. Yukino-san was celadon. Ruruka-san was lilac, and Makoto-tencho was ivory. Ah, I was apricot. The book looked great.

"But, umm . . . maybe I'm imagining things, but it seems a little too sexy . . . ?"

"You're exaggerating. But we do need a selling point."

"S-So the sexy angle was somewhat intentional . . . ?"

But Kiriya-san didn't respond. He acted like he heard nothing and continued to prepare the booth. I know, the book had to catch the buyers' attention, but I felt we shouldn't be too hung up on sales, either. Kiriya-san might have his own ideas, but I wasn't convinced. However, since he'd produced the books all by himself, I couldn't complain too much. Hmm . . .

"Well, let's do our best." Kiriya-san smiled.

We began to sell our books.

"Please take a look. Hi. It's a book with maids!"

As we called out to the people passing by, I found out we had a lot of downtime at the booth. According to Kiriya-san, most people lined up at the larger clubs first thing in the morning, while small groups like us would get attention in the afternoon. I quickly grew bored of the lulls, so I started people-watching. There were a lot of strange people to look at. Wow, these cosplayers have so much presence. Maids stand out, I thought, but not like these cosplayers. Oh look, there's a maid with broad shoulders, thick chest and legs, and a buzz cut . . . it was a male, of course. These "maids" were definitely different. Oh wow! Were those little girls running around in one-piece school swimsuits? Wasn't it illegal to do that in Japan? There were a lot of people carrying around a lot of stuff. Wait . . . is that guy really going to take home the plastic bag with the rosy-cheeked anime character striking a slutty pose in a skimpy outfit? Someone should stop this pervert. M-Maybe his mommy didn't pay enough attention to him . . . ?

"Can I see your stuff?"

"Wh-What?!"

I finally noticed a customer standing in front of me. "Umm, er, uhh, where's the sample book . . . umm . . ."

"Here you go."

Yes, I should have handed him a copy like Kiriya-san just did. Thanks. I couldn't react fast enough because he caught me off guard and I was coming down with a fever.

Wow, a customer was actually flipping through our book. This was exciting. The silence was killing me, though. I was glad to have someone read our book, but I'd have been happier if he bought it, too. I wonder if he's going to buy it. Or is he going to put it down and leave? Oh, look, he's fished out a wallet from his pocket . . .

"I'll buy one."

All right! We did it!

We'd sold only one book, but I was jumping for joy inside. My hands tensed as I gave him his change. I gave him the book and said, "Thank you!" It was inspiring. I wished more customers would buy our stuff!

"Excuse me."

"Oh, yes? Please take a look at our book!"

"Please give me fifty books."

"*Huh?*"

I turned around and smiled, but the number he had asked for was astonishing. I heard of people buying in bulk, but this much? On top of that, he was a foreigner. Was there a maid fad happening in his country? I couldn't believe it.

"U-Umm, do you really want fifty books?"

"Yes, fifty."

Unsure, I looked at Kiriya-san. But Kiriya-san calmly

grabbed a pile of books and said, "That'll be twenty-five thousand yen, please."

"Thank you."

All I could do was watch with my mouth open.

Comiket was full of surprises.

As Kiriya-san predicted, more people began to crowd around our booth in the afternoon.

Our books were flying off the shelves, keeping me and Kiriya-san quite busy. Get the money and hand over the change and book. It sounded like a simple procedure, but when done repeatedly, it tired you out. I started to feel a little faint, probably because of the rising fever.

"I'll take one."

"Sure! It's five hundred yen!"

"Here you go."

A high school boy handed me a 5,000-yen bill. Oh gosh, I told him, we're running low on bills, so I wish he had a smaller amount, but I reluctantly gave him 4,500 yen in change.

Then he stopped, checked his wallet, and said, "I'm sorry, I have a thousand-yen bill. Can I have that five thousand yen back?"

"Oh, thank you. We were running low on bills." I took his 1,000-yen bill and handed him 5,000 yen.

"Oh yeah, can you change this into ten thousand yen?"

What a needy customer. He put away 500 yen from the 4,500 yen I gave him, then added a 1,000-yen bill and the 5,000-yen bill to make 10,000 yen.

"Great. We were low on change, so getting some smaller bills helped us out a lot."

"Thank you," the boy said when I handed him the 10,000-yen bill. He turned on his heels and walked away. "No worries. Please enjoy the Comiket."

"Hey!" yelled Kiriya-san as he grabbed the boy's hand!

The boy tried to squirm out of the hold, but Kiriya-san twisted the boy's arm behind his back and controlled him. With his arm locked, the boy winced in pain.

"Ki-Kiriya-san, what are you doing?!"

"Aaliyah-san, stand back. Stay calm."

Kiriya-san glared at me. I didn't know what was happening, so I followed Kiriya-san's orders. Kiriya-san kept the boy in the armlock and asked me, "What did the customer pull out of his wallet?"

"Huh? What?"

"Think real hard. How much did he pull out of his wallet? The total number of bills?"

"U-Umm, he first pulled out a five-thousand-yen bill. He said he had a thousand-yen bill, so he gave that to me. Two bills, total."

"What did you hand him, Aaliyah-san?"

"I gave him forty-hundred yen in change, and a ten-thousand-yen bill . . . uh? Oh gosh!"

"You need to be more careful. When you gave him the five-thousand-yen bill, he only gave you a thousand-yen bill. He cheated you out of four thousand yen."

"Eh? R-Really . . . ?"

"Yes, really. He pulled a 'change' scam on you."

Kiriya-san locked the boy's arm tighter and escorted him to the staff booth.

"That boy ran away from his hometown. There are all kinds of people here, don't you think?" Kiriya-san said as he came back.

During the hour Kiriya-san was gone, I was able to sell the rest of the books. We sold out, but because of that scam, Kiriya-san and I weren't in the mood to celebrate. We just sat there in silence.

It was about 3 P.M. Comiket was about to end.

"Kiriya-san, why did you want to make a *doujinshi*?"

Kiriya-san turned to me and smiled. "I told you before. I wanted to change the café."

He flipped through the sample book on the table and continued, "In order to change the café, you need to do some radical things. You need to do new things to stimulate change. Things like changing your 'character' type, lying, et cetera . . . Oh, please don't tell the others about this."

"Th-Then why are you telling me? Shouldn't you be lying to me, too?"

Kiriya-san suddenly turned and faced me at a precarious 45-degree angle and said, "Because I'm in love . . ."

Huh?

"With you."

Wh-Wh-Whaaat!

What in the world was he saying? What did he mean? Was something wrong with him? I looked away, confused. I couldn't look back at Kiriya-san. My heart was beating faster. B-But, I'm really sorry and I hope I don't hurt your feelings, but I'm not interested in you, Kiriya-san. At least I wasn't supposed to be. No really, I wasn't, I think. But why was my heart beating faster and faster? The world was spinning around like I was sitting in a Teacup ride at a theme park. I nose-dived into the ground. I was a ball of light flickering on and off like popcorn, and fading in and out. Oh no, what was happening . . . ?

"Aaliyah-san? Aaliyah-san?! Are you okay?!"

A maid down—knocked out by a fever and carried out on a stretcher was an eerie sight to behold.

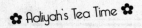
❀ Aaliyah's Tea Time ❀

January 16   Comiket Master

Great job at the Comiket! Our staff booth was in the same row as yours. I was wearing a staff band around my arm. Do you remember me? I hope you participate in the next Comiket!

January 17   Aaliyah

I had a great time at Comiket! I apologize for causing so much trouble.... I'm so embarrassed.

Comiket Master, you're a staff member? I was wondering what staff members do at the Comiket. I was surprised that all the staff members were volunteers. What do you do, specifically?

January 17   Comiket Master

I have an answer to your question! ^_^

First, we help with the setup the day before the event. We carry in desks, tents, and other props and lay them out. A lot of staff members aren't used to hard labor, so many of them are exhausted by the end of the day. (LAUGH) On the day of the event, we split up into many different s—entrance staff, public area control, sales support, customer service, export sales, industry liaison, change room staff, hall staff, first aid, record-keeping, medical clinic, international relations, media liaison, etc. Even the staff members don't know all the different s. I was in charge of the entrance area, but I yelled so much, I almost lost my voice by the second day. ^_^

The hardest Comiket I ever worked was the summer Comiket during a typhoon. The parking lot space used for the general admission line was flooded. The attendees were struggling to keep their shoes from getting wet, but it couldn't be helped, so I kept yelling, "Your shoes will be soaked! Please give up!" Of course I was drenched from head to toe. I had a bad fever for a whole week. ^_^

January 20   Aaliyah

Some things weren't meant to be funny, but . . . I'm glad to see that people other than maids have a service spirit.

January 20   Yukino

We want you to come work at our café. You'd make a great replacement for Aaliyah—

⇨ **January 20   Aaliyah**

Oh, no! Please don't give up on me!

9

A Maid's Day Off

(Tsundere Café Battle Story)

Thump, thump, thump. I shoved my feet into my favorite pair of boots and flew out of my apartment to go downtown. It was cold outside, but the sky was clear. I wanted to hum a song. I felt great because it was my day off!

The hippest way to spend a day off is to go to the streets of Akihabara, of course. Making rounds, visiting, patrolling, wandering . . . call it whatever you'd like. On my days off, I like to explore places I usually walk past on my way to work, like other maid cafés and popular stores. Also, it gives me a chance to observe how the people of Akihabara truly feel about maid cafés, so this day was both business and pleasure for me.

Today, I wanted to visit . . . oh wait, I should eat first. A warrior with an empty stomach cannot fight, nor journey through the streets of Akihabara. My favorite meal was a cheese ramen served at a local dig in a JR train line underpass. I loved the unusual combination of cheese and ramen kicking and popping on my tongue. Okay! Let me buy the meal ticket from the vending machine in front of the store. . . .

"Aaliyah-san."

"W-Whoa! You scared me!"

"What are you doing?"

Ah . . . oh my God! I pushed the wrong button! I pushed the seaweed ramen by mistake. . . .

"What's wrong?"

"Why, you! You deprived me of my cheese ramen!"

I grabbed the unwanted seaweed ramen ticket and turned around to see Kiriya-san in his everyday clothes. He was smiling ear to ear as he watched me losing it in front of the ticket machine.

"O-Oh, hey, there!"

"Good afternoon. Is this your day off, Aaliyah-san?"

Argh . . . Kiriya-san was all cool, calm, and collected, as usual, but I wasn't sure how to react to him after his confession at Comiket. Running away in any direction was probably the best option.

"Hey, aren't you going to eat here?"

"N-No, I won't. My cheese ramen turned into a seaweed ramen, so I don't feel like eating anymore. I'm just going to wander around Akihabara, so you don't need to tag along, Kiriya-san. See you later . . ." I stammered, then turned on my heels to run.

I tried to get away, but . . .

"Umm, Kiriya-san, why are you following me?"

"I'm free today," Kiriya-san said, and smiled as he took long strides and stayed right behind me.

"But, you know, I just wander all over the place randomly, so you won't find it any fun being with me."

"That's fine. I can always take off if I get bored."

Gosh, I wished he hadn't said that. I'd be the bad guy if I

totally rejected him at this point, so I guessed I'd have to take him around to a few places before I faded out or something. . . .

"So, where did you want to go first?"

And so, Kiriya-san tagged along on my precious day off.

Regardless of whether or not I had a weirdo tagging along, I had a mission to accomplish. I walked past the gauntlet of salesmen promoting their electronics shops and honed in on a particular shop with a wooden sign propped up.

"TODAY IS *TSUNDERE* DAY"

Yes, my mission was to go to a café with a special, limited-time-only *tsundere* theme.

Tsundere . . .

There are probably many guys who've grinned after hearing this word, like carnivorous beasts salivating over a platter of meat, but I'm sure there are a few girls innocently batting their eyelids like deer in the headlights, wondering what the term means. Let me give a brief explanation. *Tsundere* is a new, exciting term, freshly created for our times; it was defined in *Basic Knowledge of Modern Terminology* (fact) and also published in a research paper titled "*Tsundere* Digest" (fact). Please record this word into your brain with a permanent marker!

Er, ahem . . . those who have a *tsundere* character are often stubborn and aggressive (*tsun*), but sometimes sweet and gentle (*dere*). It's that type of girl who acts all tough, has hysterical fits, and gets overexcited about things in order to mask her true feelings toward the boy she likes . . . but still sometimes reveals tenderness toward him: a very charming, or *moe,* character! The bigger the gap between *tsun* and *dere,* the better the *tsundere.* Of course, the word is based on the kind of girl who can't ever seem to express her feelings of love openly, so that when this type of girl, say, tries to give a special boxed lunch she prepared to the boy she's crushing on, she'd probably say something like: "Oh, are you eating bread that you bought from a convenience store? Why do you eat so much junk food? You need to eat a balanced meal. Gosh, you don't take care of yourself. Here, have this boxed lunch instead. I-I didn't make it for you. I just made too much. Oh, goodness me, you don't need to thank me. Just shut up and eat it. But . . . thank you . . . for eating everything."

You shouldn't do something you're not used to. (Blush)

I hope my explanation of *tsundere* made sense. Kiriya-san and I were now just about to enter a café full of waitresses who are acting in the *tsundere* style, pioneering a totally new style of service!

"Welcome to . . . Hey, why are you here?"

As soon as Kiriya-san and I stepped foot into the café, a double-ponytailed waitress pouted her face and welcomed (?) us. Wow, a real *tsundere*! The waitress was happy that we came to the café, but she couldn't express it properly. She was a really good actress. (This is my ESPN play-by-play commentary!) Her hesitant speech and mannerisms were so adorable. She led us to a table in the far corner and said, "I guess I have to show you to your table . . . b-but I'm doing this because it's my job, that's all. Here, sit in this corner and shut up. You better take your time [she said in a tiny little voice] and enjoy yourselves."

The *dere* finally came out in the end! Folks, this was what we call a true *tsundere*! I'm stoked. I'm moved to tears. I had a hard time hiding my smile. When Kiriya-san and I sat down, the waitress brought us some water and said, "I give water to all the customers, okay? You guys aren't special or anything. C'mon, stop staring at me and give me your order already."

Wave after wave of *tsundere* action continued. I never imagined the *tsundere* play to be so perfectly choreographed. I've heard about little sister cafés and BL cafés, but these specialized-character cafés might become mainstream someday.

"Kiriya-san, you need to speak up soon and order, or else the *tsundere* waitress might get angry . . . ^_^"

"Why are you so rude to customers?"

Bffft!

I almost spit out the water I was drinking.

. . . Er, ahem. I was so shocked I looked all super-deformed like a manga character, but oh well.

"Kiriya-san, the waitress was just playing out a character. This café specializes in this type of service . . . !"

"Stop that attitude. It's disgusting."

I tried really hard to explain the situation to Kiriya-san, but he completely ignored my comments and lectured the waitress instead. He said that her attitude sucked, and she was downright rude to customers. Was she serious about her job? Kiriya-san shared a piece of his dense mind with the poor waitress.

"I'm sorry. . . ."

O-Oh gosh, this was supposed to be a *tsundere* café, but the waitress was apologizing for real . . . !

"I'm glad you understand. You can go now."

Kiriya-san waved her off, huffed his nose in disgust, and gulped down a glass of water. He commented, "What a pain."

Actually, *you're* the pain . . . in the rear.

Gosh, what the heck was wrong with him? His royally conceited attitude lacked common sense . . . no, but it was within accepted Akihabara norms. I sensed it every now and again, but Kiriya-san had an extremely snotty attitude, and his ego was as high as the moon. A smiling, highly tolerant and forgiving partner usually balanced a harsh *tsundere* to create a peaceful atmosphere. But if you paired up a *tsundere* with someone with zero patience or tolerance (like Kiriya-san), tragedy unfolded. . . .

W-Well, I figured I should get rid of the source of my headache but that first Kiriya-san should do some soul-searching and reexamine his callous behavior.

"Listen, just because she ticked you off doesn't mean that you just blow up at her. You need to learn some people skills and hold back a little!"

"Hold back? Hrmm . . ."

"Yes, at least have the patience to tolerate a genuine *tsundere.*"

Oh, the exact opposite of a *tsundere* is the "honest-cool" character. Maybe Kiriya-san is one of them? Honest-cool characters are always very honest and cool-headed, and reveal their feelings and thoughts openly at the drop of a hat. They're upfront and direct about liking or hating someone . . . I think.

"No can do. I can't stand rude people."

Correction. He's not an "honest-cool," but a "blunt-selfish" guy. Or maybe a "conceited-cool" guy . . . a character who never compromises his wants and needs, but is instead quick to blame others and point out their faults. A troublesome character indeed! My things are mine, and your things are mine, too. If you don't have food, get out of my face and starve to death. The king had donkey's ears, so he couldn't hear the people's voices!

"Uhh, Aaliyah-san? Did you sigh?"

Of course I did! He was the biggest pain in the butt I've ever met.

"You're so kind and gentle at work, so why are you so self-centered and egotistical when you're not working?"

"Work is work, so I just do what is asked of me."

Argh . . . forget it, I give up. Whatever. It's my day off, so why should I waste any more time on this idiot? Oh, look, the waitress brought our tea. It saddened me greatly that we're at a *tsundere* café but the waitress was acting normal because of Kiriya-san. *Boring!*

"See, at least the tea tastes wonderful."

"The tea at our café is better quality."

"*Ignore him . . . ignore him . . . I don't want a selfish king's comments to ruin my relaxing tea time. It's just an empty echo. White noise.*" The tea was wonderful, the background music was soothing, and it felt warm and wonderful.

"Oh, yeah."

Yes?

"You haven't answered my question from the other day."

Bffft.

I spurted out a mist of tea from my mouth.

Cough, cough! "Why'd you bring that up now?"

"Because I wanted to know. I told you my feelings at the Comiket. If you forgot, I'll say it again. I'm in love with you."

"Gosh, don't say it here!"

"Why not?"

Oh gosh, mighty king, don't you care what you say around your lowly peasants? He was too blunt! He irritated the crap out of me. I never imagined Kiriya-san to be such an ignorant jerk. If I was an evil drill instructor, I'd throw a bunch of war gear on his back and torture him with a death march to hell. I'd belittle him by yelling, "Go home and suck your momma's breasts!" and toss him into a freezing river. I'm the Maid Machinegun!

. . . Oh . . . no, no! Even though he rubbed me the wrong way, or even if I hated him as much as a cave cricket, or even if he ruined my delicious tea . . . as a maid, I should never belittle anyone, even on my day off. I had to endure it. Withhold my anger. I should meditate to calm my soul.

"Well, I know you won't refuse."

Eeeek!

Enough! I was fed up. Kiriya-san, get out of my face already! Be gone! My biggest pet peeve is guys bothering me on my precious day off. I wasn't sure I could restrain myself any longer. I might go postal. I hope he's stabbed by my maid unicorn horn and dies. I should crack his head open with my killer right hook!

"Whoah, there."

"Wa-Wa-Wah . . . ouch!"

He swiftly dodged my punch, and the momentum caused me to tumble from my chair. Oww, I felt a stinging pain in my knees and the cold stares of the other customers.

"Are you okay?"

"I don't need your help, Kiriya-san!"

I swatted Kiriya-san's hand in disgust, slapped some money onto the table to pay for my tea, and ran out of the *tsundere* café.

Phew! Kiriya-san had ruined a perfectly good day. I sat on the street railing and looked down at the ground. The exciting hustle and bustle of Akihabara made empty background noise overhead. To make things worse, I had to work with Kiriya-san at the café tomorrow. How depressing. I had played an important role in hiring Kiriya-san, so I couldn't possibly talk bad about him at the café. I was totally bummed out. . . . H-Huh? My cell was vibrating. I had a text message.

See you at the café tomorrow. Kiriya

Snap.

The sound of my cell phone snapping in half echoed through the streets of Akihabara.

Argh!

A Maid's Dimly Lit

Counseling Room

What have you written recently?

Was it a love letter, confessing your love to someone? Or a short e-mail to greet or encourage someone? Sometimes written communication is more effective than the spoken word. A message can sometimes have more impact with the pen than the voice.

With that in mind, our café placed message notebooks next to the cash register to provide more interaction with our Masters. We had a notebook for each maid. The Masters were encouraged to write something in the notebooks at their tables, and the maids wrote their replies after work. It was similar to an exchange diary, increasing communication between Masters and maids. You may have already figured it out, but "Aaliyah's Tea Time" pages were actual entries pulled from my café notebook.

As of about two months ago, I wanted Masters to send in their concerns and worldly problems to me. I was immediately bombarded by online entries from Masters and Mistresses asking for help. The problems ranged from light problems like what to eat for dinner to serious relationship issues. I read each entry carefully. Hmm, many of you had a lot of anxiety and stress bottled up. This might sound brash, but it felt good to have many Masters depend on me. Oh, we even had a grandfather who sought advice on what sort of birthday present to give to his grandchild. It was delightful. *Tsk.*

. . . Which is a lie, of course. I haven't received squat from anybody. I say again, I received no freaking e-mail whatsoever!

Wh-Wh-Why didn't I get anything?! (Ripping the corner of a handkerchief with my teeth.)

Er, sit down. No, kneel. Listen. Here is a maid offering free advice to people from the goodness of her heart, yet no one has sent me a single lousy e-mail. Are you guys out of your mind? Is it morally correct to pass by a maid offering selfless love? Ignoring her is worse than rejecting her outright. Not acknowledging the presence of a maid is depressing, cruel, and evil. It's as inhumane and torturous as Makoto-tencho ordering, "Do some overtime, please! ★"

But I won't lose this battle. With love, courage, and a true service spirit, I'll (forcibly, if necessary) provide advice to my Masters' problems! Even when unwanted, the million-watt passion of a maid persists. If I'm knocked down, I'll dive forward. And I won't give up until I use up all my ammo!

I promised God that I would get to know my Masters' problems, through my own personal efforts, and placed my bets on my message notebook. Hmph, they say you can't put your arm through a sleeve that doesn't exist, so . . . if God doesn't exist, I'll just have to make one up. I erased the title on the notebook cover, "★ Aaliyah's Tea Time, ★" and replaced it with "A Maid's Dimly Lit Counseling Room." My notebook was thus transformed into a problem-solving book of advice.

A few days later . . .

Lo and behold, my notebook was filled with problem after problem!

Tsk, tsk. The Internet can't beat a sincere handwritten note. My handwriting isn't all that great, but I did my best to answer each plea for help with all my heart. Problems ranging from what to eat for dinner to bankruptcy because of large debts kick-started the Maid's Dimly Lit Counseling Room! Let's begin with a problem posed by Fried Tofu-san (pseudonym) from Tokyo!

Q. I'm thirty-two years old and married. Recently, my wife has been behaving in a very strange manner. She wakes up in the middle of the night to eat raw butter, leave the house, and wander to the Inari temple. She fills our refrigerator with fried tofu (we ate fried tofu for dinner every night this week). When she sees me, she gets on all fours and makes a threatening pose. When I try to talk to her, all she says is "Koon."

A. This is more of a monster-hunting request for Hell Teacher Nube than personal counseling. But let's try to look at this problem from a maid's perspective. You need to consider it from a new angle. A paradigm shift of sorts. First, look at the costume shops around you. It should be easy because there are a lot of costume shops in Akihabara. You'll see a lot of outfits and accessories, but buy the most expensive furry ear and tail attachments. Add a pair of furry paws, too. When you get home, put them on your wife.

Now look at the miracle! She looks and acts like a fox!

Take advantage of your fox-possessed wife and transform her into the world's most authentic cosplayer impersonating a fox. I'm sure your wife will enjoy her new furry look, and as long as you are comfortable with her transformation, you'll regain your happy marriage. Actually, I think she acted that way as payback because you secretly patronize maid cafés every day. You should beg her for forgiveness. But thank you for always "coming home," Master!

Great! Oh wow, I might be able to save the world after solving all these problems. Maybe I've evolved from a personal counselor to a divine oracle? Okay, let's see the next troubled person! Hmm . . . from Tokyo . . . huh? Kiriya-san?!

Q. I have a crush on a girl. I've expressed my feelings to her several times already. But for some reason, she acts like she hates me. I think she doesn't realize her true feelings for me yet. She shouldn't deny what's in her heart. Please drop the act and admit your love to me.

A. If there was a key on the computer that could beat this guy senseless, I'd use it in a heartbeat.

This concludes my personal counseling session! I'll never do this again!

January 30   Seeking advice

Good afternoon. I always read your essays. I know you don't plan to have any more counseling sessions, but can you please help me with my problem for the last time?

Recently, I've lost interest in real girls. I no longer feel attracted to three-dimensional (3-D) girls in real life. But I love anime and manga girls with a passion. I'm obsessed with two-dimensional (2-D) girls all day long. Basically, I wish I could marry xxxx (manga character name deleted). When I tell my friends, they look at me like I'm a rotten hermit crab or something. But I believe 2-D girls are just as alluring as real-life girls. What should I do? I look forward to advice from a maid. Thank you.

January 31   Aaliyah

You have a "2-D Complex" or a "2-D-con." Umm ... maybe you can rehabilitate a little at a time by getting used to real-life girls. Maybe I can help. Please come to our café!

January 31   Makoto

There isn't anything to "fix." If "Seeking Advice" is self-sufficient, then he should live as he pleases.

January 31   Yukino

If you're only interested in 2-D girls, then I wonder why you come to our café. Maybe you still feel attracted to 3-D girls. I suggest you think through your feelings and figure out what really turns you on.

January 31   Ruruka

You're a hero. A savior. An emperor. Conduct Kumbhak (Yoga breath retention) underwater and liberate yourself to reach nirvana. Just stick your face in a bucket of water and stop breathing for ten whole minutes. When you see a beam of light, you will reach the land of God. Persist. If ten minutes doesn't work, try doing it for twenty minutes—no . . . how about an hour? If that doesn't work, jump from a high cliff. (BLACKED OUT) (Erased)

January 31   Aaliyah

I-I think you'll do just fine! Even if you don't, you'll be okay!

Save the Café?

Recently, I've noticed fewer Masters "coming home" to our café. . . .

Actually, the weekends are busy as heck, but the café seems emptier on weekdays than usual. We maids seem to have longer pauses between customers, and we have so much more time to polish cups and glasses for the second or third time around. We keep trying to fill the lonesome periods with repetitive tasks.

"Hmm . . ."

Even Makoto-tencho's sighs, her nose buried in the logbooks at the end of the day, sound distressed. Hmm . . . this is bad. If we lose many more customers, the café might go bankrupt and close down. If that happens, then we'll become vagabond maids . . . !

Shudder, shudder . . . We can't depend solely on Makoto-tencho to save the café. Keeping a maid café afloat requires the collective effort of all the maids. We mustn't forget the creed, "One for all, all for one" (like the Three Musketeers).

But I've come up with an idea. We should have an Events Day!

- - -

Events Days are a big draw at maid cafés.

Some Masters swear by it. Events Days certainly are popular attractions. It's nice to "come home" on a regular day, but it's also quite refreshing to see maids dressed up in different outfits for certain themes or concepts. The maids will try to come up with many different Events Days, so the variety is endless and the dream expands. Little Sister Day, Priestess Day, Nurse Day, *Yukata* Day, China Dress Day, Goth Loli Day, School Swimsuit Day, *Zettai Ryoiki* Day, Halloween, Christmas, New Year's, specific manga/anime characters, et cetera . . . For example, School Swimsuit Day is so popular that the federal government operations were affected . . . er, ahem . . . just kidding. Please strike the last comment.

Unfortunately, there are more than a hundred shops that sell maid outfits and other costumes, so a lot of the Events Day ideas are seriously played out. But wait! I told myself. If we can find an exciting, original idea, we can shine in a saturated market and get our tiny café back on the map!

So I set up an idea box in the break room to solicit new ideas for an Events Day. If three people put their minds together, I figured, then we'll end up with a lost herd . . . no, I mean we'll get true wisdom. Maids shouldn't just sit around all day and wait for things to happen. We need to be more proactive and strive for victory! Maids should have an Events Day for the maids, by the maids, and with nothing but the maids, so help me God! Okay, so what ideas were dropped into this box? Oh, this is an industry secret so please don't leak this information out!

MENTAL HEALTH DAY (Contributor: Name withheld)

- Mental Health Day where all the maids go nuts.
- When a Master comes home, the maids slit their wrists to spurt blood and pass out.
- The maids will cheerfully greet, "Welcome home, Masters! ★" while they lie on the ground with dead eyes. The contrasting voice and body language creates an eerie feeling.
- Each Master will be given a knife, fork, and razor blade.
- Everyone is too scared to read about "Today's special: Drug overdose." Unfortunately, that is the menu special every day.
- A maid with exorcist skills presides.
- Plus a maid with supernatural powers.
- The maids eventually make life-threatening mistakes, but try to pass it off as just being "clumsy girl characters."
- Maids kill one another over their favorite Master.
- Of course, the Master receives collateral damage.
- Splash piping hot tea on a Master, flail knives and frying pans as you wildly run about, kill all the Masters with a hidden machinegun, burn the café down, and commit suicide. On top of that, a mysterious virus spreads from your charred body and infects all of Akihabara like a plague.

Umm . . . Ruruka-san, can you please come to the break room for a "friendly" conversation?

Gosh, I'm trying to get everyone involved to help the café, so I don't appreciate these ridiculous pranks. Ruruka-san doesn't seem to understand that our café is in crisis. Her destructive ideas are quite insulting to the other maids who gave their honest input. See, Ruruka-san needs to listen to these sound suggestions by other maids. . . .

Maid Guy Day (Contributor: Anonymous)

• An Events Day with guys wearing maid outfits.

• Café is filled with macho men as servers.

• When a Master comes home, the guy maids greet, "*Ossu!* Master!"

• They certainly aren't full of charm, but full of harm.

• All dishes are made of heavy steel to help maintain their buff bodies.

• People die when they order "Today's special: Fighting Spirit Injections." Unfortunately, that is the menu special every day.

• The trademark quote of guy maids: "Hope you can withstand our manly services!"

• In order to find the most macho guy maid, we'll conduct the World Maid Guy Tournament.

• Of course, the Masters will receive collateral damage.

• One day, a group of bad maid guys called the "Four Heavenly Gods" will attack the cafés across Akihabara. Good maid guys will gather to defeat the bad maid guys. They will fight the bad guys for seven days and nights. Not only do the bad guys run away, but Akihabara will be obliterated.

Y-Yukino-san, please come to the break room for a "friendly" conversation!

Huff . . . huff . . . huff . . . pardon me. Don't worry. I immediately removed these foolish suggestions by my senior maids from our idea box. Gosh, I'm trying to get good ideas to save the café, and they turn in nothing but half-baked ideas, or worse, sick jokes.

But . . . I feel as though the other maids aren't aware of what a crisis we're in. Am I the only one who understands how dire the situation is? Or maybe I'm just completely overreacting? No, no, I don't think so. . . .

"Aaliyah-san?"

"Y-Yes!"

His voice gave me a real jolt. I saw Kiriya-san standing behind me. Argh . . . I guess Kiriya-san is my last resort. Since he was a customer until recently, maybe *he* has a great idea. I'll look past Kiriya-san's totally annoying, self-centered ego. Sure, a drowning person is desperate enough to grasp at straws to survive, but there's another saying about someone who got rich by starting off with a single straw.

"Events Day?"

"Yes. Events Days are all so similar and bland, so we need to come up with a striking new concept that will blast a fresh, inspiring wind through the oversaturated maid café industry. An Events Day concept radical enough to revive our café and shoot our revenues through the roof!"

Kiriya-san squinted his eyes for a bit and said, "I have an idea."

"Great, what is it?"

"If we can pull it off, it'll be a definite success. The customers will rush to our café by the thousands. And we will surely be the talk of the industry."

"Wow, what sort of dream project is it?"

"We don't have to prepare anything special. We don't need to advertise it much, either, because it'll spread by word of mouth like wildfire."

"Really?! It really is a dream-come-true Events Day isn't it! So what is it?"

"When the customers enter the café, the maids are . . ."

"Okay, the maids are . . . ?!"

". . . naked."

I was struck dumb.

"Nude Day. It'll be a hit, for sure."

I was still speechless.

"Our café will be overloaded with customers. The only problem is how to deal with the police."

I believe this café has finally reached the bitter end.

Tea Break ☞ A Senior Maid's Soliloquy

It's time to execute my plan.

After I confirmed that the break room was vacant, I turned on Aaliyah's laptop, which she left out on the table. I easily passed through the persistent user confirmation screens with a list of passwords I acquired ahead of time. As a word of advice, Aaliyah should hide her hand movements when punching in her passwords to prevent others from breaking in.

I'm doing this during the busiest time of the day—lunchtime. The maids are too busy to poke their heads into the break room. My shift starts at 1 P.M., so I have a full hour to tinker.

Let me introduce myself.

I'm Yukino.

I'm a waitress working at a café in Akihabara, and senior to Aaliyah Kominami, the actual author of this book.

I have a quick question for the readers.

Have you ever wondered what Aaliyah, the writer of this essay, is *really* like?

I know she shares her thoughts and ideas on this site. She's eighteen, works at a maid café in Akihabara, and is an *otaku* who enjoys drinking different kinds of tea. Her profile isn't generic, but I suppose it isn't all that unique, either.

But as her coworker, I'm not convinced this profile describes her well. I'm not saying that she's lying or anything. I just think that something about her personality, statements, and behaviors aren't typical of a "part-time worker in Akihabara." After reading through her initial string of essays, several places raise doubts or questions in my mind.

First, she mentions this "service spirit" thing a few times, but don't you think she must be exaggerating?

Second, aren't there *too many* quirky characters around her?

Third, isn't her Japanese a little weird at times?

Fourth, why is she even writing this thing?

I'm sure some of you readers wonder why I'm invading her site out of the blue and accusing her of being suspicious. Maybe you think I'm out of my mind or something. Fine. Let me explain. I know the truth. Even the reason why she became a maid wasn't "normal" by any means.

It all started last year.

Though Aaliyah acts as a job interviewer for the café now,

back when she was hired, we didn't conduct interviews. It began on a rainy, chilly day. A young girl, running out of breath, entered our café during our downtime.

"Welcome home, Miss."

I greeted her at the door. A breathless customer, much less a female customer, was quite unusual, but maid café employees wouldn't last long if they were taken aback by that sort of peculiarity. I serviced her according to standard procedures (not that our café has any manuals stipulating standard procedures, mind you) and led her to a table.

"B-B-B-B-Black currant tea . . ."

The girl stuttered. As water droplets trickled down her wet strands of hair, she nervously stared down into the amber surface of the tea, the steam clouding her face. Even a stray cat picked off the street would relax, but she was locked up in fear.

Half an hour later . . .

The girl remained in that position and didn't move whatsoever. Of course, the tea went cold. Her nervous aura must have scared the other customers, because they left the café, one at a time. Eventually, she was the only customer left, with us maids standing in the corner.

I finally decided to check on her. Maybe she had come to make a complaint about the café or something. Determined, I walked toward her table.

Like an animal, her ears perked up at the sound of my footsteps. She cautiously twisted her head toward me. I stopped in my tracks. I never expected these words to come out of her mouth, though. . . .

"Me work. Master happy. Me maid. Okay. Yes?"

Why was she speaking bad Japanese like some foreigner selling jewelry at Ueno Station?

Even now, her Japanese is still pretty eccentric, but back then, her weird Japanese, coupled with her extreme nervousness, resulted in her being almost incomprehensible. But she tried her best to communicate her thoughts. It took a lot of effort to figure out what she wanted to say, but in simpler terms, she was trying to tell us this: "I want to work at this café."

It just so happened that at that very moment we were looking for a new part-time worker. The maid café business wasn't booming back then like it is now, so the cafés were actually struggling to find new maids. But should we hire such a bizarre, inexperienced girl to work at our café . . . ?

But I had no authority to make that decision. Makoto-tencho did.

I called Makoto-tencho from the kitchen and explained the situation. Then she listened to the girl asking in her peculiar fashion for the job. Makoto-tencho silently stared at her pleading face, but eventually said, "Let's work together to make this a great café, okay?"

All the employees, including myself, went slack-jawed at this surprising decision. We had actually been wondering how Makoto-tencho would let her down gently, but instead, the exact opposite happened! To tell you the truth, Makoto-tencho's behavior is still a mystery to all of us. She is probably the café's most unpredictable person.

Of course, the girl was overjoyed.

Aaliyah was so happy that her eyes spun wildly, and she finally dunked her face into the cup of tea.

I wonder how this episode would have read if Aaliyah had narrated it in her unique way. I'm sure the readers would have found themselves pulled through the story and overpowered by her extreme enthusiasm. But let's analyze this objectively. There were so many weird things happening, and everything seemed so wrong. Yes, ever since she appeared in our café, I've not been able to shake my suspicions about her.

I suppose there are some readers who don't believe me and doubt my opinions, so let me describe another incident.

Do you recall a customer named Ozuma-san?

He was a customer who came to our café like clockwork. He came every other day, drank coffee, and stayed for only twenty minutes. He gathered detailed data on our café, was initially tailed by Aaliyah but dragged her around instead, and in the end gave her a Steiff Teddy Bear present as an overeager token of encouragement. But after that incident, he never showed up at the café again.

If the story ended there, then one would conclude that he was just an eccentric man. You might have passed him off as just a strange, socially maladjusted guy who did nothing more than add a little spice to Aaliyah's site.

But let me disclose one thing Aaliyah isn't aware of.

Ozuma-san still frequents our café.

He temporarily stopped coming to our café for a while, but since Kiriya-san has begun to work at our café, Ozuma-san has come back to visit several times. He doesn't come as frequently anymore, but he still drinks coffee and leaves in exactly twenty minutes.

Apparently, Ozuma-san comes to the café *only* when Aaliyah isn't working.

I'm probably the only one who's made this peculiar connection. Ozuma-san is visiting the café while taking care to avoid Aaliyah. I'm sure of it. Somehow, Ozuma-san has gotten access to our work schedules. Many readers might assume it's easy to get a café's work schedule, but we're talking about a maid café. We do not readily disclose our employees' schedules to just anyone.

If my essay is published, then Aaliyah will know my suspicions toward her. What will she do and say in response? Will she act like she never read it?

But everything will help to crack the mystery about her.

I've known Aaliyah for more than a year now. Hopefully, I've earned her trust as a coworker, and I sincerely care about my junior maid like I would a younger sister. My objective definitely isn't to destroy my relationship with Aaliyah.

But there's no time to worry about sentiments now.

There is a scant possibility that I'm just crying wolf. But if that's true, maybe it would be better for all of us.

Even so, my sixth sense is telling me there's something about Aaliyah I can't ignore.

After spending more time at the café with Aaliyah than with my family or lovers, I still can't solve the mystery behind her. As I wrote this essay, I dug through all the files in her laptop, but couldn't find any data that could reveal her identity. So I concluded that maybe I could use this essay to crack the mystery.

I'd like those of you reading this essay to carefully observe her future actions. I wonder what will come out of Pandora's box . . . an ogre, a snake, or nothing at all. I conclude this essay with a sincere wish that my adorable junior maid is as innocent as her appearance suggests.

IMPROMPTU INTERVIEW: ASK THE MAID!

Amid the mob of people in Akihabara, I walked alongside Murakami-san, my agent.

I visited various maid cafés in Akihabara both as research for my job as a maid and as my personal hobby. No matter how cold the wind bit into my skin, I would move forward on the path to become an expert maid. Today, we were going to visit one of the more established, famous maid cafés, Café Mai:lish!

. . . Or so we thought. We became utterly lost in the streets of Akihabara. I initially led my agent confidently, boasting that I knew the exact location of Café Mai:lish, but after second-guessing myself, not sure whether to turn at this corner or the next . . . we wandered around without a clue and got ourselves lost.

"Should we ask the maid over there?" Murakami-san suggested.

As I grabbed my head in despair, Murakami-san approached a maid on the street, handing out flyers. I'm sorry that I seem to have such a formidable talent for getting lost!

Hmm, what's going on? Murakami-san was engaged in heavy conversation with the maid. I thought he was only asking for directions . . . . He even handed her his business card. What . . . oh gosh . . . the maid was coming this way!

"Are you Aaliyah-san?" she asked.

"Uh, yes, I am Aaliyah, I suppose."

"Wow! Nice to meet you! I'm Nano Endo!"

"N-Nice to meet you."

I was surprised to know that not only was Nano-san a former Café Mai:lish maid, but that she also reads my online essays! Oh my gosh! This was the first time I met a fan who read my stuff. On top of that, a fan who was also a maid! What luck!

At that moment, an awesome idea flashed through my mind like lightning!

"Umm, Nano-san, do you have some time?"

"Yes?"

"Can you help me? I have a favor to ask you."

Yes, during my research on ways to improve the maid café industry, a chance encounter with Nano-san was a blessing from the skies indeed. As a maid striving to improve myself at every opportunity, I wasn't going to miss out on a chance of a lifetime . . . to do an impromptu interview with a senior maid! Nano-san happily obliged. This was a dream interview between two maids. Well then, I present to you the deepest of all in-depth maid interviews. Please sit up straight, listen carefully, and enjoy!

✧ It Was Sweet As Cotton Candy T_T

AALIYAH: Nano-san, as a senior maid, please teach me anything and everything!

NANO: Please ask away! What would you like to ask me, Aaliyah-chan?

AALI: First, how long did you work at Maid Mai:lish?

NANO: About two years, I guess. It felt a lot longer because I did so much while I was there. In fact, I started working there at its initial establishment.

AALI: Establishment?

NANO: Yes, I was one of the first people they interviewed and hired. When I started, I thought everything in the café was all planned and ready to go, but it wasn't. We had to figure out how to set the table, where to stand, et cetera. I think we were eventually able to give the place a homey atmosphere.

AALI: Gosh, that *is* painstaking. I joined my current café well after its establishment, so I was never involved in that process.

NANO: Well, I don't know why our café didn't already have set rules. There are stores with their own policies, you know? For example, Anna Miller's shops and McDonald's franchises have procedure manuals that specify everything. I think a lot of maid cafés have manuals now, but does your café have a manual, Aaliyah-chan?

AALI: It's not written, but instead passed on verbally from senior to junior maids. My seniors were so strict that I sometimes felt compelled to cry in the middle of Akihabara.

NANO: Oh, I think I made a few of my junior maids cry, too. ^_^ But we want our junior maids to toughen up and improve! Actually, I think you were lucky to have a strict superior who made you cry. You need to understand *why* your seniors are so strict when they're teaching you the café's secret rules.

AALI: Oh, I see. If I had time to cry, I should've instead been thinking about why they were so severe! ^_^

NANO: I guess there are reasons behind every procedure that is determined by the café. Whether to greet customers with "Welcome to our café" or "Welcome home" and such, you know?

AALI: So why does Café Mai:lish use "Welcome to our café"?

NANO: The image we had for Café Mai:lish was either "an estate-like café with maids" or "a cosplay café with maids" . . . so we decided to use "Welcome to our café" . . . so basically, though Café Mai:lish had "maids," they still functioned more as waitresses than maids. So we thought of our café as "a cosplay café with waitresses dressed as maids." Oh . . . but on Maid Day every Tuesday, they are really "maids," so they'll greet their customers with "Welcome home."

AALI: Oh, so your café focuses more on cosplay than maid service.

NANO: Tuesday is the only day they will provide full maid service because they are cosplaying as "maids."

AALI: There are a lot of maid cafés, but you're saying that a maid café and cosplay café are different in principle?

NANO: Yes, I think it all boils down to determining the

main objective of that particular café, Aaliyah-chan. It depends on what your café wants to specialize in, either as a cosplay theme restaurant or an authentic "maid" café and such. I hope you take your senior maids' statements to heart and also read between the lines. Who is the strictest senior in your café?

AALI: Yukino-san, I think.

NANO: How so?

AALI: She's evil . . . like a mean platoon sergeant. . . . (trembling with fear as she says it).

NANO: ^_^ What does she personify in relation to the café?

AALI: The strictness of the café, I suppose . . .

NANO: ^_^ Where does the strictness come from?

AALI: I need to figure out the underlying reason for the strictness, right? Umm, I suppose behind all that toughness, there's a whole lot of love . . . or maybe something warm and fuzzy. . . . I'm sorry, I'm totally winging it. ^_^

NANO: Behind all that strictness, you'll find the true objective, or concept, of the café.

AALI: I thought it was simply a maid café, but I never put much thought into it, I suppose.

NANO: Being a real maid is tough enough . . . but I believe "cosplaying as a maid" seems just as hard, if not harder. I mean, you're acting out a role, after all. Aaliyah-chan, when you see a customer enter the café, what's the first thing that crosses your mind?

AALI: Welcome home. I want the customer to feel comfort as if they came home.

NANO: That's where you're wrong. Yes, you're saying,

"Welcome home." But if that was their real home, it's understood that they'll come home. It's not their real home, yet they go out of their way to "come home" to your café.

AALI: You're saying that our café has a special attraction that a real home doesn't? There's a secret?

NANO: Yes. Your greeting "Welcome home" must include a feeling of appreciation or "Thank you!" for the customers. Do you have that feeling in your greetings?

AALI: (looking down, with a fading voice) . . . I'm kicking myself already. I'm so stupid!

NANO: ^_^

AALI: My head is like cotton candy . . . sweet and fluffy, but empty. I feel as if you've knocked some maid sense into me.

NANO: I guess. ^_^ Okay, first strike. Sorry, I hypothetically slapped your right cheek.

AALI: I suppose my left cheek is open for the next blow. . . . ^_^

NANO: My last blow will make your face swell so bad that you can't work at the café for a week!

AALI: After a week of recovery, I'll have a golden maid heart!

NANO: I hope so. ^_^ Well, this is my way of training junior maids. I'm sure other maid cafés have manuals that teach employees how to serve customers, from the appearance of their uniform to shaping their hearts and minds.

AALI: You're saying you can become a maid by following many different paths! That's deep.

✧ A Maid's Heart Is
"an Organ Full of Eternal, Boundless Love"

Nano: With a strict senior maid, you'll surely attain the secret to becoming a maid with a heart of gold.

Aali: I'll become the ultimate maid!

Nano: Aaliyah-chan, you probably aren't sure of how to reach your ultimate goal of becoming a maid because you're not sure if you should refine your shape or your form first to reach your desired final state.

Aali: Sigh, this requires a lot of thought. What should I watch out for?

Nano: First, greet customers properly. Second, greet customers properly. And there are no third or fourth, but the fifth is to greet customers properly. (Basically, start with a proper greeting and end with a proper goodbye.)

Aali: Roger that. I'll repeat this mantra ten times a day. ^_^

Nano: Having personal conversation skills is secondary, like a toy prize in a cereal box. Yes, toy prizes are important, and some people even throw away the cereal to collect toys. But if the cereal company sold toy prizes without the cereal, it would be pointless, just like a café that can't service a customer properly. It'll just become a regular restaurant that happens to employ talkative waitresses. A "maid café" can't exist without maids.

Aali: Right, it'd be just a plain old café!

Nano: Though you have to put more feeling behind your greetings "Welcome to our café" and "Welcome home,"

you also need to put real feeling behind questions like "Would you like some water?" as well.

AALI: "A maid's heart is a whatchamacallit heart!"

NANO: ^_^ A heart full of maternal love is natural, but a "maid heart" is man-made.

AALI: If I harden my fragile, glass maid heart into a steel maid heart, then I can move forward. ^_^

NANO: Only you can harden your own maid heart. Why did you want to work in a maid café, Aaliyah-chan?

AALI: I was attracted to the role of a maid.

NANO: Role?

AALI: You know, sensing a customer's need and fulfilling it, and in turn being fulfilled by the fact that you satisfied the customer . . . a beautiful role where my heart was . . .

NANO: "An organ full of eternal, boundless love"?

AALI: Actually, I like to call it "an organ full of maid love."

NANO: Sweet! Since you have such a clear objective, then your next step is to make it real!

AALI: I'm rushing ahead, like an out-of-control steam locomotive! *Toot toot!*

NANO: You might blast through a few red lights and run over some people, but, oh, well . . . ^_^

AALI: Please look the other way.

NANO: (LOL) How many maid cafés did you apply at, Aaliyah-chan?

AALI: Just the café I work at now. I practically forced my way in.

NANO: I see.

AALI: That's why I really appreciate my coworkers and manager.

NANO: You're lucky that you fit in with your café. Currently, there are so many girls wanting to become maids who can't. Why did you choose that café in the first place?

AALI: I previously went to that café as a customer. I remember the maid who provided great service. I'm sure the maid at that time thought nothing of it, but I was deeply moved by her wonderful service and made my decision to apply on the spot.

NANO: Is that maid still working there?

AALI: Yes.

NANO: May I ask who it is?

AALI: The super-strict Yukino-san.

NANO: Oh, the evil platoon sergeant. ^_^ Well, gee, your objective is right in front of your face then!

✧ THE PRETTIEST RIBBONS IN AKIHABARA

NANO: What type of uniform do you wear at the café? At Mai:lish, the uniform has multiple pieces, so depending on the theme or situation, you can mix and match items to dress like an orthodox English maid or go to a looser cosplay style. I sometimes wore a light blue maid outfit.

AALI: Our uniform is an orthodox English maid outfit, but we have a few one-piece variations. We're allowed to choose our favorite.

NANO: So your outfit designs follow the basic pattern, with no cosplay variant pieces?

AALI: Yes, that's right. We wear the orthodox outfits, but it's hard to keep the white parts clean because they get dirty so quickly.

NANO: Right. There's the problem. If it's hard to get dirty, then what's the point of trying to stay clean? The more effort you put into staying clean, the more attentive you become. You need to understand why you're wearing such a high-maintenance outfit.

AALI: Oh gosh, I have no maid knowledge whatsoever. . . .

NANO: The easiest to dirty is a white maid apron, right?

AALI: We actually suggested a black apron, but white aprons are the standard according to a TV show I saw the other day.

NANO: Absolutely. I think I saw that TV show also. Keeping the white apron spotless is paramount!

AALI: So the key to a maid mind-set is so close by!

NANO: Yes. You'll see things all around you, if you only pay attention. Do you wear aprons, lace, and frills?

AALI: We have lots of lace.

NANO: Do you iron them? And wash them?

AALI: (in a small voice) Our senior maids do it for us.

NANO: What about you, Aaliyah-chan?

AALI: (in a smaller voice) Sometimes . . .

NANO: That's not good enough!

AALI: Y-Yes, I'm sorry!

NANO: Geez! Time to slap your left cheek! ^_^

AALI: Ouch, my left cheek!

NANO: When I worked at Mai:lish, there was one thing I was proud of at our café: I believe we wore the prettiest ribbons in Akihabara.

AALI: The prettiest ribbons . . . ?

NANO: The way to make a ribbon pretty is to wash it, iron it, and starch it often. There is a technique to ironing lace and frills without flattening them. Are you doing that, Aaliyah-chan? Or do you leave it to your senior maids?

AALI: I'm kicking myself again.

NANO: *Tsk.*

AALI: I'm still *green*! I'm such a bad maid . . . a no-good maid! Please slap my cheeks some more!

NANO: *Tsk, tsk.* It's been a while since I quit Mai:lish, but I still enjoy training the young ones! ^_^ Aaliyah-chan, you can retaliate, you know. . . .

AALI: No, you're overpowering me with every blow. After you slap both of my cheeks, I don't know if I will be able to make it as a maid anymore.

✧ THE CAFÉ'S MAIN ATTRACTION IS MENTAL COSPLAY?

NANO: Aaliyah-chan, if I hadn't run across your "Maid Machinegun" essays, I would have never known about your maid café.

AALI: It's a secluded shop, not as well known as others in Akihabara, and quite barren. Please come to our café and teach us how to increase our profits.

NANO: Okay. I'll be a personal adviser and think about what will work for your café.

AALI: Thank you.

NANO: First, we should find the main attraction of your café.

AALI: Main attraction? We need to come up with one, quick!

NANO: Sure. Back when Mai:lish was established, it was easy to find because we were one of only a few maid cafés back then. The first maid café was the Cure Maid Café, which set the standard for all maid cafés.

AALI: So, the Cure Maid Café was the pioneer maid café?

NANO: Yes. Orthodox maid outfits, customer service, and a policy of keeping maids in the background, behind their Masters. It was a standard-setting maid café.

AALI: An orthodox style in which maids stayed in the background when servicing Masters.

NANO: From there, you need to find a new style. Don't duplicate. Devise a different style.

AALI: Do more cosplay, perhaps?

NANO: Maybe.

AALI: We should advertise the unique aspects of our café. We shouldn't be satisfied at being one of the many maid cafés that have occasional Events Days.

NANO: A new café needs to be remembered for specializing in something unique in order to establish some sort of reputation.

AALI: I see.

NANO: Even a bad reputation makes a café well known.

Even Mai:lish was criticized several times in the beginning.

AALI: What kind of criticism?

NANO: Complaints about some of our flashy outfits not being "maid-like" and such. In comparison, the maids at the Cure Maid Café weren't focused on any characters, didn't have name tags on their uniforms, and didn't publicize their profiles. The maids at Mai:lish publicized their profiles and illustrations of themselves. But some of the customers slammed us for trying to make idols out of maid waitresses.

AALI: Gosh, if I was slammed like that, I'd probably give up. ^_^ But does a bad reputation really make a café famous?

NANO: Suppose there's an X-axis and Y-axis. Cure Maid and Mai:lish were on the opposite sides of the X-axis. But a particular C Café went on a totally different axis. The customers were pleased with "lots of skin exposure!" and such. ^_^

AALI: Oh, that legendary shop . . .

NANO: Though that café was similar to Mai:lish in the way it created maid "characters," Mai:lish never resorted to flashing skin or adult themes.

AALI: By covering the body, it actually stimulated the customers' imaginations.

NANO: Yes, we stimulated their minds.

AALI: Mental Maids!

NANO: Or mental cosplay, to be more accurate.

AALI: With mental cosplay, the customers were encouraged to fantasize.

NANO: It makes the customers think about the café. But it wasn't just fantasizing. The customers thought deeply about our café.

AALI: Argh, since you already slapped both of my cheeks, please karate-chop my head this time!

NANO: *Tsk tsk.* They "thought about" our café. In order to direct the way they thought about our café, we had to think of the overall image of the café. We had to unify our image first.

AALI: So, all the maids had to agree to a unified image of the café for the customers.

NANO: Do all the maids in your café share a unified image of the café?

AALI: (in a small voice) I might be disrupting the unity somewhat. But each senior maid is unique. In a good way, the café seems like a zoo . . . but in a bad way, the café seems like a zoo. Everyone is in their own spheres, I suppose.

NANO: A zoo is fine. So your café has many unique characters! Mai:lish was also a zoo of sorts. ^_^ But it wasn't dangerous like a safari park, with vicious animals roaming about.

AALI: Oh, so not having a saleable concept is our café's biggest problem?

NANO: Exactly.

AALI: I'd like to come up with a new concept for our café, then. I actually wrote in my online essays about brainstorming some ideas for an Events Day. . . .

NANO: Have you discussed this with your senior maids?

AALI: Sort of . . .

NANO: "Sort of" is not enough! Is there someone in charge, such as a café owner, manager, planner, or anyone with some authority involved?

AALI: We have a café manager, but she's mostly hands-off, though spontaneous at times.

NANO: Then the waitresses and maids need to be more proactive. Running a maid café requires teamwork. At minimum, the maids need to have a unified game plan.

AALI: One for all, all for one . . . The café will improve with this mind-set?

NANO: Yes. And everyone needs to treat customers not as one of a group of customers, but rather as precious individuals.

AALI: I see. Your words are inspirational.

◇ THE FAILED PLAN FOR A "FEMALE NINJA CAFÉ" ^_^

NANO: Aaliyah-chan, your essays are entertaining and show how much you think about things. But you don't seem to include a lot of conversation with your fellow maids. Like Kiriya-san, you know?

AALI: Yikes.

NANO: Since Kiriya-san is new to the café, how about setting up a welcome party for him?

AALI: A welcome party?

NANO: Doesn't your café hold welcome parties for new employees?

AALI: Oh, we totally forgot about that.

NANO: That's bad! It's important to open up communication between maids at every opportunity and maintain a consistent image for the café. To be specific, you should have maid meetings. Personally, I prefer calling out a newbie to the back of the gym (for "initiations") . . . ^_^

AALI: So we need to establish closer relationships from the get-go. I shouldn't get carried away with Events Days. I shouldn't be wasting my time planning a "Female Ninja Café," I suppose.

NANO: Exactly. You need to build a solid foundation first. But . . . I like your idea of a female ninja theme. . . . (LOL)

AALI: When the customer enters the café, there are no employees in sight. But suddenly, from behind, a female ninja maid greets, "Welcome to my humble domain, Master." I thought it was a radical concept.

NANO: But wouldn't the customer play the role of a murder victim then? ^_^

AALI: Huh? Oh, my!

NANO: Unless the customer was a Master who controlled the female ninja.

AALI: In my concept, I suppose the customer would get killed next. "I'm behind you . . . ," then slash! The order of events would be "Customer enters, ninja appears out of nowhere, and ninja slashes customer."

NANO: That's so wrong! (LOL)

AALI: Okay, so my "Female Ninja Café" concept is a total failure.

NANO: Another problem surfaced with this concept.

AALI: A lack of communication.

NANO: Yes. Even the "Female Ninja Café" would have

been shot down by someone in your café before you went too far. In this case, I'm sure Yukino-san would have asked, "What is the customer supposed to do?"

AALI: She'd slap both of my cheeks at the same time until I came back to my senses.

NANO: (LOL) Whack! It's not just common sense, but maid sense! Of course! ^_^ I'm worried about your welfare, Aaliyah-chan. ^_^

AALI: I will endure any pain to become the best maid ever!

✧ BEFORE THINKING ABOUT EVENTS DAYS

NANO: Aaliyah-chan, you mentioned that you chose to work at your café while you were in Akihabara. Are you an *otaku*?

AALI: I'm not sure. I once tested myself with one of those "How *otaku* are you?" quizzes.

NANO: Okay.

AALI: According to that quiz, I was fifty-three percent *otaku* . . . "somewhat *otaku*." Not quite a full *otaku,* but not quite a non-*otaku* either. It seems like I'm straddling the fence or half-assed, in a sense.

NANO: Are your café patrons all *otakus*?

AALI: I think about 70 percent of them are *otakus*.

NANO: Why did you come to Akihabara, Aaliyah-chan?

AALI: I wanted to experience Akihabara . . . as a tourist, I suppose.

NANO: Did you come to buy anything in particular?

AALI: No, I first wanted to see what Akihabara was like.

NANO: How long have you been a maid?

AALI: A little over a year.

NANO: You have a problem.

AALI: Do I need to be more *otaku*?

NANO: No, that's not what I mean. Before you go off brainstorming new Events Day ideas, I think you first need to examine what the Akihabara visitors look for in Akihabara. How can you come up with a plan to please the customers without first understanding your customer base?

AALI: So you're saying I don't have enough knowledge of Akihabara.

NANO: Right. You haven't done enough research.

AALI: Oh gosh, my spine is crumbling from the maid pressure.

NANO: (LOL) Well, athletes get stronger muscles after recovering from muscle soreness.

AALI: So I'll get hardened into shape?

NANO: Something like that.

AALI: Is my maid power getting stronger?

NANO: Yes, of course. Usually, customers will seek out a maid café they had in mind already, but for smaller, lesser-known maid cafés, a portion of customers may drop in because they just happen to run across it.

AALI: That's probably true with our café.

NANO: So maybe it's important to figure out why these customers came to Akihabara in the first place.

AALI: Oh, I need to begin this research immediately. We need to understand our customers a little more.

NANO: Instead of embarking on an official research project, why not resort to local experts in your own café? I'm sure everyone in the café has specialized knowledge in some subject area.

AALI: Yes, they do.

NANO: For example, if you have an expert in BL who tells you she knows the date of the upcoming release of a BL video game, you can make plans for doing an Events Day oriented toward young women, with maids dressing in male outfits. Or if you know a particular date of an upcoming release of an adult video game, open the café an hour earlier than usual to warm up the customers who bought the game after waiting in the long, cold lines outside for hours.

AALI: So, we should provide services based on the needs of customers and current events in Akihabara?

NANO: But, Aaliyah-chan, you previously mentioned that a good maid was able to predict a customer's needs!

AALI: I'm sorry. . . . I'm all mouth. . . .

NANO: Absolutely! You've got a long way to go, young one!

AALI: I'm so inexperienced that clumsiness is my only skill.

NANO: (interjects) Clumsiness is *not* a skill!

AALI: (fades out) I'm sorry. . . .

NANO: What do you think your "character" is, Aaliyah-chan?

AALI: Yukino-san seems to have the Maid Goddess shine upon her at times, but I think only the Goddess of Comedy smiles upon my lowly self.

NANO: Why, do people laugh at you?

AALI: Umm, I don't know. They just suddenly burst out in laughter when they see me.

NANO: So, it happens to you before you know it? Really?

AALI: I suppose it's my clumsy mistakes that make people laugh at me.

NANO: (sensing something) You shouldn't call yourself a clumsy girl. Don't ever do that!

AALI: I-I'll try not to.

NANO: Mistakes are mistakes. They should never be forgiven, for any reason.

AALI: I should pack up and return to my hometown now.

NANO: (LOL) Please don't go! Everyone makes mistakes. But a maid shouldn't make a character out of being clumsy! That's the beginning of a maid's end.

AALI: Relying on my clumsiness only makes me a no-good maid!

✧ MY LIFE IS FICTION?!

NANO: Aaliyah-chan, do you just go back and forth between work and home?

AALI: Yes, pretty much.

NANO: Do you spend some time in Akihabara along the way?

AALI: I often do. I like to visit other cafés.

NANO: Oh, so you explore maid cafés? ^_^

AALI: I've been to many other maid cafés, but I suppose I wasn't noticing much.

NANO: *Tsk.* I don't think you need to go to those cafés anymore.

AALI: I'd like to use those cafés as a stepping-stone to fly to the skies. ^_^

NANO: No. (LOL) You need to look back to your *own* café. ^_^ Are you close to anyone in your café?

AALI: Ruruka-san, I think.

NANO: O-Oh, the girl from a different planet? ^_^ What do you like about her?

AALI: Well, she's close to my age. Other than the fact that she sometimes plays scary video games, I like her a lot.

NANO: Scary games?

AALI: Like the PlayStation game *Siren*.

NANO: Oh. Do you hang out at Ruruka-san's house?

AALI: Sometimes. But when I see weird stuff scattered all over her room, and hear her chant demonic spells or quote from Lovecraft novels, I hightail it out of there!

NANO: Lovecraft novels are one of the basics of becoming an *otaku,* so you should read one. In fact, it's good to know at least one of the basic *otaku* genres, like horror, because it'll help you out in the long run.

AALI: I've been trying to read a lot of maid manga, like *Emma, Kamen no Maid Guy,* and *He Is My Master.* But the more I read them, the more confused I get as to what a "real" maid should be like. . . .

NANO: Oh . . . if you consider the maid ideal to be an *eidos* . . .

AALI: Idiots?

NANO: No . . . *eidos.* (LOL) According to the Greek

philosopher Plato's concept of *eidos,* those manga present falsified forms or shadows of the true "ideal" of maids.

AALI: So, they aren't true forms of maids?

NANO: Right. You need to find out what your true maid "ideal" is and find something that closely resembles it.

AALI: So, I shouldn't be wasting my time trying to find a cool catchphrase in *Kamen no Maid Guy.*

NANO: Exactly. You shouldn't invent your own catchphrases.

AALI: Really!

NANO: Other people will find a catchphrase that defines you. Making up your own phrase is just as bad as openly advertising "I'm this kind of character" to your Masters. That's a forbidden act, by the way. And making up your own catchphrase is a no-no. Don't even go there!

AALI: As a maid, I sometimes feel like saying a phrase like "Stars in the skies, flowers on the earth, love in people, and Maid Guy for you!" But I suppose that's a definite no-no.

NANO: Wow, that's a hundred years too early for you to say. Some waitresses have profiles with illustrations, comments of people introducing her, and a catchphrase that fits her "character," but she'll never make it up on her own. People around her will notice her speech patterns or get an impression from her to get hints of a catchphrase that best describes her.

AALI: So a maid's "character" is determined by others' impressions of her?

NANO: And never by the maid herself. For example, Ruruka-san never said to anyone, "I'm from another planet," did she?

AALI: Not at all.

NANO: That's just how she is. If you were to introduce her to the café customers, maybe she'd have a catchphrase like "A quirky girl from out of this world" or something.

AALI: I see. I shouldn't try to make up my own characters. I have to rely on others to create my character.

NANO: I think Ruruka-san acts that way naturally, and her way of life is somehow fused with her maid ideals.

AALI: Gosh, you're right.

NANO: Aaliyah-chan, you seem to be obsessed with maids. But before you go there, I think you need to establish the character "Aaliyah-chan" before becoming a maid, or else . . .

AALI: I'll end up being a flat, boring character?

NANO: Sort of writing a fiction within a fiction of a fiction. (LOL)

AALI: Ohhhh. My life is fiction!

NANO: Something like a CG fan art of a crappy fan fiction of an adult game, I guess. ^_^

AALI: The original form is completely lost. . . . T_T

NANO: You'll lose sight of what's important. That's why you've been striking out so far.

AALI: I'm merely a copycat mold, imitating a fake maid image. . . .

NANO: As long as you don't get fired, you'll have plenty of time to recover. ^_^

AALI: The amount of money I owe for all those broken dishes isn't funny anymore.

NANO: Aaliyah-chan, is your café busy?

AALI: It's busy on Sundays.

NANO: When do you break dishes?

AALI: Unfortunately, it's always on our busy Sundays.

NANO: Please work hard on improving your coordination. ^_^

AALI: Should I focus on improving my skills first?

NANO: Yes. If you don't build up your basic foundation, you can't accomplish anything.

AALI: Maybe, every morning I should do squats while holding a stack of dishes!

NANO: Well . . .

AALI: . . . Am I off-base?

NANO: The way you go off on a tangent might be very "Aaliyah-like," so maybe you should analyze the way you steer a conversation away from the main subject.

AALI: If I keep following the same angle, I have a feeling I'll circle back to where I was.

NANO: By the time you make a full circle, you might be fired. Or the café might go bankrupt!

AALI: The café will turn to rubble, leaving behind a lone maid.

NANO: How many people work at your café?

AALI: Currently, five.

NANO: We started Mai:lish with seven people. The crowds never stopped coming the first week, but we were able to handle them all. Aaliyah-chan, your café could probably handle the customers with only four people, while the fifth person honed her skills. It could work!

AALI: We'll need customer service skills that will cover all the customers smoothly, from left to right.

NANO: Hmm? Don't push customers from left to right. That's rude!

AALI: (LOL) There's another slap to my cheek.

NANO: Treat each customer as an individual! Don't push customers from left to right . . . how rude! (LOL)

AALI: Maid Captain, please forgive me!

NANO: Umm, if you're just a girl who daydreams about maids, that's fine. You just don't need to be a maid, that's all. ^_^

AALI: Argh . . . I'm such a no-good maid. Please beat me senseless and punish me! (LOL)

✧ IF THE YOUNGER SISTER LIKES YAKINIKU, THEN I LIKE SHABU-SHABU!

AALI: Nano-san, what should our café become?

NANO: To me, Mai:lish is the best maid café ever, so I'm not sure how to answer your question. . . .

AALI: You were enthralled by your own charming café. (LOL)

NANO: I did all I could before I "graduated" the café. Our café doesn't call it "leaving" or "quitting." We "graduate."

AALI: It's different than quitting a normal job.

NANO: Once you've done everything you could at the café, you "graduate" and move on to the next phase of your life. In that sense, we want people to give their all until they've exhausted themselves, I guess.

AALI: So you want me to strive to that level of completion? And without such aspirations, I can't improve?

NANO: Exactly.

AALI: I need to gain more experience.

NANO: Yes. And remember: "One for all, all for one."

AALI: Teamwork.

NANO: Yes, absolutely.

AALI: And beyond all that is . . . graduation.

NANO: Once you reach graduation, you will truly appreciate and adore your own café, even after you leave it. If you leave a café with bitter memories, it's basically your fault for feeling that way. Aaliyah-chan, it seems like your café still has a lot of potential for you.

AALI: Well, yes, but my cheeks are so red and swollen that you can't recognize my face anymore.

NANO: Oh yes, it's swollen pretty bad. ^_^

AALI: Oww . . . Nano-san, why did you leave after two years?

NANO: I wanted to start a new chapter in my life. The biggest reason was being selected for a permanent job at a company. Sorry for bringing you back to reality, but I have a story to share with you. ^_^ My younger sister actually found a job out of college faster than I did, and she used her first cash bonus to treat me and my parents to *Yakiniku*. When she said, "Big sis, eat anything you'd like! You like cow tongue, right? Here, order the good, salted cow tongue!" I felt like I needed to support my parents just like she did! I needed to push myself to the max!

AALI: Your pride as an older sister burned you inside out, didn't it? ^_^

NANO: As a maid, I made enough money to support myself, but not my parents. I think everyone needs a period of time to neglect their parents . . . as a lesson learned, of course. But . . . I couldn't stand that my baby sister beat me to the punch! >_<

AALI: You can't lose to your younger sister!

NANO: If my younger sister treated my parents to *Yakiniku,* then I'd treat them to *shabu-shabu*! So when I received my first cash bonus, I did just that.

AALI: *Yakiniku* vs. *shabu-shabu,* the great beef battle of the century! ^_^

NANO: I told my sister, "Hey, you like *shabu-shabu,* don't you? You can eat all you want . . . !"

✧ ENERGIZE ME FOR AN ADVENTURE

AALI: So . . . what is it that makes a maid happy? If a maid can't provide for her parents as long as she's a maid, how can a maid achieve happiness . . . ?

NANO: Maids in Akihabara maid cafés can't escape the requirement to be visually pleasing. It's sad, but true. For example, there are no maid outfits in size XXXL. I don't think any customer visits a maid café to see grandmothers wearing maid outfits, either.

AALI: True.

NANO: Youth is valued . . . and especially when looks are involved.

AALI: Oh, brief but brilliant youth!

NANO: I believe working as a maid is a once-in-a-lifetime opportunity.

AALI: Yes. I'm actually living in the moment as a maid, so I know.

NANO: But if you're going to commit to it, you need to do your best.

AALI: On the flip side, only those who strive to do their best make it as a maid?

NANO: Exactly.

AALI: Are there any hiring standards?

NANO: A reliable girl . . . I guess.

AALI: Reliable girl?

NANO: Those who want to be maids for the rest of their lives aren't cut out for it. Maids need to achieve the goal of being a maid early on, and also have a vision beyond their life as a maid.

AALI: A post-maid life . . .

NANO: Cafés are looking for a girl like you, concerned about balancing your maid job with your life goals of "taking care of your parents" and "life beyond a maid."

AALI: That's a strict standard.

NANO: Yes, very much so.

AALI: So, how about girls who want to achieve everything at once?

NANO: I know a few girls who are total workaholics. They put in a lot of effort to maintain their looks. Of course, a maid's income alone cannot support a family, so they'll take on other jobs, such as being convention booth girls, writing magazine articles, and doing other odd jobs. The amount of effort they put into finding and continuing to receive extra jobs—which don't pay too well, so they'll do many jobs in a month—is phenomenal.

AALI: It's hard to maintain a maid's good looks. An arduous task.

NANO: These girls work multiple jobs without compromising their excellent customer service skills, solicit to get more jobs, and somehow support their parents—they're insane. I didn't think I could hack it!

AALI: You couldn't seriously commit to the maid job as a long-term project.

NANO: Right. I didn't have enough guts or dedication to commit to it.

AALI: But you don't know if you can make it or not unless you try it. You'll realize it once you become a maid, though.

NANO: Absolutely.

AALI: Why did you want to take on a new job as a "maid in a maid café" in the first place?

NANO: I saw a want ad for my maid café during college, and thought, *Hey, that's a new type of job*. Back then, I wanted to take on all kinds of challenges. And it also sounded . . . interesting. ^_^ Until then, I was living a safe, mundane life. It was my last year in college, so I was willing to make a small gamble before graduating.

The possibility of Mai:lish falling on its face in failure lingered in my mind, but in the end, I think I won my bet. It was really fun.

AALI: So, you decided to go on a brief adventure?

NANO: Yes, before I graduated. But of course, there will be many adventures ahead of me, and many more chances to disappoint my parents. . . . ^_^

AALI: But you wanted to take your chances just this once. You stood up and charged ahead.

NANO: I thought, If I don't venture now, when will I ever? I was a bit desperate, I guess.

AALI: Please energize me so I can venture out, too!

NANO: Aaliyah-chan, didn't you already make your jump into the adventure?

AALI: I jumped, but I don't know if I have enough heart to continue. T_T

NANO: But you've survived a year already. ^_^ After seeing my younger sister beat me, I ultimately returned to a normal life, but I had an exciting two years, taking the biggest chance of my lifetime and doing everything I ever wanted to as a maid. ^_^

AALI: So, you were left with a refreshing feeling of accomplishment?

NANO: Yes!

AALI: Oh, I just felt a fresh breeze blow through my barren soul!

NANO: I'm glad!

AALI: Thank you for the interview today! I'll continue to do my best!

12

A Super-Producer's Explosive Debut!

I arrived at the café way before it opened and fought through a pile of research papers in the corner of the break room. The TV was turned on to the Sunday morning superhero shows for kids.

"Adventure Ranger *Boukengers*!"

Yes, I was definitely going on a bold adventure.

After recovering from Nano-san's mix of harsh words and encouragement in the interview the other day, I wasted no time in sharing my thoughts directly with Makoto-tencho. With my newly opened eyes full of hot passion and my heart full of renewed determination, I headed straight to Makoto-tencho.

"Aaliyah-chan . . . a producer?"

"Yes, absolutely. You need a super-producer to help make the Events Day, the main attraction of the café, a success. Of course, I know I'm not a full-grown maid. But even though I'm not a mature maid yet, leading a production might aid in my growth. I don't want to rely on you and Yukino-san for everything and end up being an inferior maid!"

"Okay. Go on."

"Yes, I know: My idea will be trashed immediately. But

when you consider the current dire situation of the café, I believe a bold, suicidal move . . . no, an adventurous decision to use me as a producer, is necessary. Even if my odds of success are ten percent, I'm willing to stake my maid life on it . . . huh?"

"I said okay. But make sure you show me the project plan before you execute it."

This was how I somehow slipped through as the producer of an Events Day project.

Now that I was chosen for the project, I had to come up with a project plan, pronto. Depending on the project, I could produce an Events Day theme that lasted as little as a day or two, or as long as a week. My deeply hidden maid heart began to spin its gears. What kind of event should I do?

Tsk! If it was the previous me, I'd yell, "Time to do some research!" and bolt out into the streets of Akihabara, only to return with my tail between my legs and no results whatsoever. But not this time around! The new Aaliyah would not step on the same nail again. After Nano-san's interview, I put myself through grueling training in voice projection, observation, walking, bowing, tray holding, and cash register operation to improve my maid skills. I had my evil senior maid trainer, who has no blood in her veins and is incapable of crying, but has a hundred percent pure maid heart, drill me to death. I'll withhold the trainer's name based on her request, but her name starts with "Yu," has "ki" in the middle, and ends with "no." Now that I had enhanced maid skills, my maid brain went on full turbo to reach the divine truth of my Events Day plan.

The key theme for the maid café event is the *moe* genre!

Moe is the ultimate key. Many of you may not have noticed, but maid café events and the *otaku* industry's *moe* genres are very closely related. For example, the little sister *moe* manga/anime characters led to the establishment of Little Sister Cafés. *Tsundere* characters brought out *Tsundere* Cafés. Maid *moe* characters brought out maid cafés, of course. All these popular events had one thing in common— the characters or themes originated from *otaku* genres!

Now that I knew this, I had no time to waste. One of the Eight Cardinal Rule of Maids: If there's something wrong, hurry up and fix it. *Moe* is a feeling of being charmed, but I wanted to categorize the different types of *moe* and find an effective event that would blow a fresh wind into the stagnant maid industry. There are more than a hundred forms of earthly desires, and just as many *moe* genres, but I removed those genres that were too common or too extreme, and analyzed the compatibility of the remaining *moe* genres with our maid café. Also, just in case there are people who are totally oblivious to the *moe* boom, you may use my notes as a course in *Moe* 101, so please peel your eyelids back and pay attention!

• **Childhood friend *moe***

A *moe* genre in which a character feels *moe* toward a childhood girlfriend as they grow up together. The type of girl who would storm inside your bedroom to wake you up for school, clean up your room on her own, or eat dinner with your family almost every night: you know, your ideal childhood friend. We won't include the grim aspects of the real-life childhood friend who hangs out with a gangster boyfriend and stops talking to you for ten years or something. The only problem with trying to act out this *moe* genre comes up when we are forced to greet a new customer, "Thanks for coming. After all, we hung out together for years. But . . . umm, wh-what's your name?" It's pretty awkward to serve new customers with this theme.

• **Magical girl *moe***

A *moe* genre in which a girl uses magic or is transformed by magic. The girl usually changes outfits with a particular spell or chant, and has an animal sidekick who can speak the human language. The main appeal is the fantasy or mystical aspect . . . but it isn't the type of mysticism where a stage magician pulls a rabbit out of a hat or anything. Oh, but if it helps, I can fake my accidents with "Oh gosh, my magic went berserk and broke the teacups!" . . . Okay, you didn't hear me say that.

• ***Tsundere moe***

I already described *tsundere* in chapter 9, so I won't repeat myself. The bigger the gap between *tsun* and *dere*, the larger the *moe* factor. The other day, a women's gossip magazine covered this topic. Also, a few new subcategories of *tsundere* have recently sprouted, such as *tsuntsun* (no *dere* at all), *deretsun* (the opposite order of *tsun* and *dere*), *nin-*

dere (a ninja with *tsundere* qualities), and *bushidere* (*bushi* [samurai warrior] with *dere*). The latter outgrowths came out quite randomly, but people who are interested in them should check them out. The more information I gather on this genre, the less I know whether or not it's feasible for use in a café.

• **Robot** *moe*

A *moe* genre in which you feel *moe* toward a robot. This genre seems minor, but in reality it is somewhat popular. If Honda could only use its world-renowned robot technology to build maid robots to man the café, it would be awesome, but unfortunately, it lacks the appropriate technology, justification, and money to realize this project. I could easily put a cardboard box on my head and greet my customers, "*I am a maid ro-bot, Mas-ter,*" but Yukino-san would probably put me in a chicken wing armlock, so this genre is a no-go.

• **Doll or puppet** *moe*

In this *moe* genre, which surfaced within the past few years and which is quite similar to robot *moe*, you feel *moe* toward a humanoid doll or puppet. Decorating the interior with figures and dolls might liven up the café, but if a customer requested, "I want a doll to serve me," we would have to put a cardboard box on our head and say, "*I am a doll, Mas-ter.*" This would trigger another chicken wing armlock, so I should stay away from this genre.

- - -

. . . Hmm, I've introduced a few genres, but it's hard to pick the right *moe* category because it has so many subcategories. Other genres include girls with glasses, cat ears, clumsy girls, rich girls, younger sisters, older sisters, mothers, girls with illnesses, ghosts, monsters, gods, multiple personalities, amnesia, emotional trauma, dysfunctional family, and so forth, and so on . . . an endless array of genres. I have no clue as to which genre will lead our maid café to success. Maybe I should combine a few and go wild, like a "Younger sister with glasses wearing cat ears and with a life-threatening illness but who actually is a monster *tsundere*" Events Day or something. Just like the motto of the legendary Tiger tank, the thickest-armored and strongest firepower of World War II, "Large tanks will blow away small ones," maybe we should package several *moe* genres together and beam the customers up to *moe* heaven as fast as a bullet train. Prepare to fire! Fire! Blast them away with the 88-mm cannon. N-No, stop. That was my idea up until now. This insensitive and shallow idea came from my previous no-good maid self. The interview with Nano-san made me aware of that. I need to come up with a new strategy. Please watch over me, Nano-san. "I will become a brilliant maid soon!" I vow to the shooting star with the most respectful salute! (Note: Nano-san is still alive.)

"What is this?"

"Whoa! Kiriya-san!"

Before I knew it, Kiriya-san had arrived at the café and was standing right behind me. As I stood there, saluting to a big pile of papers, he sighed. Something is wrong. "Wh-

While I was brainstorming some ideas for the Events Day project . . ."

"Oh, you were acting a little weird."

Argh, he sure knows how to rub people the wrong way. Kiriya-san showed no interest in my research papers on *moe* and walked past the piles of paper to prepare the café before we opened. Hmm, these days, Kiriya-san seems irritated . . . or cold. I'd finally researched *moe* genres and almost come up with a bold plan for Events Day, but . . .

"Well, these ideas are just rehashes. A lot of places already have these events."

Gosh! He ruined my lovely morning with his royal higher-than-thou attitude. Why the heck does he assume the world revolves around him all the time? He keeps acting like a snotty king—wait . . . king?

"What's wrong? You have a weird look."

"I got it! A king!"

"Huh?"

"Not 'huh'! A king!"

That's right! I was so lost in the *moe* genre that I almost forgot the true meaning of maids. A maid's primary mission is to provide her Master with the best service possible. Maids were most glorious during England's Victorian Era. Yes, we'll make a café with maids providing the finest British service to the customers, who are nineteenth-century nobles . . . in our "Victorian Café"!

"Sigh. The Victorian Era? Are you serious?" Kiriya-san muttered.

"Gosh, can you please share my excitement? Instead of a

single maid providing all the services, we should split up the various roles. House maids, kitchen maids, parlor maids, and those in male outfits will be butlers and footmen. We'll decorate the café to replicate nineteenth-century England—within our budget, of course—and make it members-only. It'll be a social spot for ladies and gentlemen of nobility. We'll serve British desserts, such as pudding, scones, plum cakes, and biscuits. I can finally make good use of my English conversational skills with customers."

"Hmm, is that so," Kiriya-san mumbled.

"Yes, every customer will be treated like royalty." Capable producer Aaliyah Kominami's Victorian Café project will succeed! All that's left is for Kiriya-san to change his attitude and cooperate!

13

A Maid's Secret Sigh

"I'm taking a break."

I announced this to Makoto-tencho and left out the back exit. My afternoon break was a great time to unwind after the wild lunch rush. I left the café during a slow period and ventured downtown.

But . . . people were looking at me for some reason. Every person I passed did a double take. What was going on? It was weird. Maybe people realized my name "Aaliyah Kominami" could also be read as "Goddess of Beauty"? Sorry, just dreaming (instant apology). But people were seriously looking at me. Did I look strange or something . . . ?

Oh, I'd forgotten to change out of my maid outfit!

Oh my gosh! I usually changed clothes before I went out, but the maid outfit had started feeling so natural on me that I didn't notice the difference. Technically, maids shouldn't wear their maid outfits outside the cafés, but it seemed like such a a pain to return to the café, so . . . I-I figured I could at least take off my white brim and apron to be less noticeable. I'd take it off temporarily. I wasn't going far, so my one-piece dress would be fine.

I heard there was a store near Kanda Shrine that had good

sweet sake, so I decided to try it. I usually ate lunch during this break, but . . . I hadn't had much of an appetite because I'd been worried about a lot of things.

It was only two weeks before my "Victorian Café" opened.

I couldn't sleep at night, so I fell asleep during the day. . . . No, I mean, I pulled an all-nighter and wrote up a plan that Makoto-tencho finally approved. It was a weeklong event, so I continued to research and prepare for it. The concept was for customers to feel like British royalty. The café interior wouldn't be Buckingham Palace or anything, but we'd do what we could within our limited budget.

Because we weren't ordering in bulk, some of the items used for this event were a bit pricey. Specially ordered cups and saucers might become a hit, I figured. Of course, I also ordered the tea varieties preferred by Englishmen. I was still deciding on what desserts to serve.

Oh, the biggest feature of this event would be the variety of different outfits maids would wear in the morning and afternoon. Traditionally, British maids changed outfits throughout the day. In the morning, they wore plain dresses while they completed the day's tasks, but at night, they entertained guests during social events in more formal wear. Following the same fashion, our maids would switch outfits between day and night, allowing customers to come to the café two times in one day and see something new each time. Of course, we needed to acquire new maid outfits, which is quite difficult.

Err . . . can you tell that my troubles weren't really about the event? A producer is heavily responsible for a project in general, but I really enjoyed the process of planning this whole thing.

Well, I don't want to admit it, but I'll tell you what's been bothering me.

Quite recently, our café started a new system suggested by Kiriya-san.

A tip system.

Of course, the maids don't negotiate tips with the customers or anything. Masters are given a few "tip" tokens as they enter the café, and give tips to the maid who provided the best services to them that day. The Masters can then take pictures with the winning maid. By the end of the day, the maid who's won the greatest number of tips is recognized as the "Maid of the Day." This new system has been an unexpected hit, attracting many customers.

But the maids themselves haven't been too thrilled with this.

Last Sunday, an overwhelming number of customers poured into the café at the start of this new event, causing the maids to rush around in a mad flurry. And it didn't help that we didn't have enough silverware. Even running our dishwashers full-time, we couldn't catch up with the demand. I sensed something was wrong, so I peeked into the back kitchen.

The dishes were sitting piled up all over the kitchen!

In order to earn a tip, the maids all stayed in the main hall where the Masters could see them. Of course, if you helped out in the back, you had no chance of getting a tip. As a result, all the maids were hanging out in the main area, overcrowding the usually clean aisles.

Oh my gosh! Maids who preferred to help in the background like little fairies or dwarves now ignored the dirty dishes piling up and competed for tips in the main area.

But . . . at least the café increased profits.

Let me point out that the tip system isn't bad. A little competition between maids isn't unhealthy, either. But I wonder if this event really matches the image of our café, or if this is the best way to conduct this event. At this rate, our quality of customer service will drop. The comforting atmosphere of the maid café will turn into a vicious battleground filled with frantic maids fighting for customers. It's a huge problem!

But . . . it's quite embarrassing . . . it makes me blush. . . . My maid ranking, according to the tip scale . . . has blasted to . . . rock bottom. I'm the worst maid. Doom!

To make things worse, even though it's supposed to be a ranking of maids, Kiriya-san, a *male* employee, is at the top. The reason why he gets all the tips is because he monopolizes the female customers. He's the only guy, so it's only natural that he gets all the tips from women, but my sorry behind has tumbled to the bottom of the popularity chart.

In other words, if I dared to complain about the tip system, it would look like I was just jealous of Kiriya-san's top post. As much as I hate the entire situation, I have to leave it as is. One for all, all for one . . . I guess.

But I overheard something the other day.

It was after closing time.

When I was cleaning up the main hall, I heard a voice from the break room. I walked toward the room to hear the conversation, but I stopped in my tracks.

It sounded like Kiriya-san was talking with someone on his cell phone.

I knew I shouldn't do it, but I put my ear on the door to listen to his conversation. I didn't know if he was talking with a friend—I could only hear Kiriya-san's voice. I couldn't hear everything he said, but he did utter some shocking phrases.

". . . I'm not having fun at this job."

It seemed like he was venting about the job. He sounded irate and fed up. He sounded colder than usual, and that brought shivers down my spine.

". . . we need to end it soon."

Moments later, Kiriya-san hung up. I rushed back to the main hall and continued to clean, but my heart was beating hard. What in the world was going on? I thought Kiriya-san contributed to the café because he enjoyed working here. But his statements and tone of voice had indicated otherwise.

What was the ace employee of our café up to? And what could a bottom-ranking maid like me do for the café? Nothing? Oh gosh . . .

As I got lost in my thoughts, I finished off my sweet sake. Time passed as I sat on the store bench outside and stared at the traffic. W-Whoa! I finally noticed a grandmother sitting next to me. Uh, well, it's not that I didn't want her to sit next to me, but she surprised the heck out of me.

"Umm, good afternoon!" I said.

"Good afternoon. What a cute outfit."

"Oh, thank you!" I hastily replied. The grandmother smiled. Her compliment made me all warm and fuzzy inside.

"Where do you work? A department store?" asked the grandmother, as she looked at my one-piece dress.

"No, I don't work at a department store. I'm a maid. Umm, I'll try to describe it in simple terms, but I guess I'm like a house servant or female attendant, you know? This occupation was most prominent during the Victorian Era in England, from the latter half of the nineteenth century to the early twentieth century. In Japan, Osamu Dazai was attracted to female attendants in cafés, and the Imperial Navy had female attendants wearing maid outfits in their officer clubs. And in the past few years, the ultimate maid outfit rose out of the ashes! Oh, uhh, sorry. I spoke too much. But maids are really popular these days. Haven't you seen one before, ma'am?"

But the grandmother answered, "No, not really."

Argh . . .

There are many non-*otakus* who've lived in this area surrounding Kanda Shrine long before Akihabara was known as an *otaku*'s sacred gathering place, a promised land, and Shangri-la. And these people, like this grandmother, probably don't give a damn about Akihabara or maid cafés.

I wasn't sure how to contain my excitement, or what to do with my feelings.

Looking at it objectively, being a maid café waitress was getting to my head. Because of all the attention I received from customers, I was under the illusion of being someone important.

But I never meant to get all conceited or to think of myself as a "maid imitation."

I couldn't back down now.

I shook away bad thoughts from my head. My break was over.

"I must go, ma'am! Please visit my café, okay?"

"Okay. Take care, dear."

I ran back to the café. Please don't tell anyone I left the white brim at the sweet sake shop . . . okay?

March 14   Figurine *moe* tribe

I'm looking forward to the Victorian Café. I have an idea.

How about making figurines of the maids in your café? You can sell them during the Victorian Events Days, Aaliyah-san. I think it'll sell well. I'll definitely buy some. At least a hundred!

March 17   Aaliyah

What a wonderful idea! If we combine the rising fad of figurines with maid cafés, it's like giving an iron club to an ogre, or a mop to a maid . . . a force multiplier, for sure. Using Japan's world-renowned man-ufacturing skills, let's do a "Maid of the Week" figurine series. Let's make something we can present at Japan's largest figurine event, the Wonder Festival, also known as Won-Fes. Customers who order tea will have a chance to receive a free figurine. We can make figurines that advertise the unique qualities of each maid!

March 17   Ruruka

At 2 A.M., the "1:8 Bloody Aaliyah" figurine will let out a bloodcurdling yell as she shakes and rises from hell. . . .

The hair of "1:8 Cursed Makoto-tencho" will eerily grow one centimeter per day. . . .

The "1:8 Wandering Yukino" will put a curse on you if you leave it in the same place for more than three days. . . .

The "Actual-Size Neck-Slashing Ruruka" will try to kill the owner to take over her soul. . . .

And what looks like a garage kit (put it together yourself) or cut-up body parts actually needs no setup . . . the "1:8 Mutilated Kiriya" . . .

March 17   **Aaliyah**

Scratch that! We can't use this idea!

14

Where Are the Maid Cafés Going?

♫ Look to the skies of Akihabara . . . the sound of boot steps . . . unwavering . . . oh maids . . . oh maids . . . wobble wobble . . . whump.

As if a 100-ton shackle weighed down my feet, I slugged around the super-busy café. Argh, I hadn't gotten enough sleep, so I had a major headache that felt like a hammer was banging my head. My eyes were dry, and I had no appetite. Life as a maid by day and a producer by night began to chip away at my supposedly invincible heart. On top of that, after the introduction of the tip system, the mood in the café turned ugly. The tensions between the maids were strung tight like a piano wire stretched between steel poles. We got so lazy that we only washed dishes after we received a Master's order for tea. I couldn't stand it any longer, so I went to the back to wash the dishes. Of course, that killed all my chances for getting tips, which kept me at the bottom of the ranking, and thus made it harder for me to object to the tip system . . . a truly vicious cycle.

But I couldn't let my preparations for the Victorian Café project slide. I had morning and evening outfits for the maids, and had already selected the English teas. I tasted the scones. The maids snickered when they tasted the scones, and Kiriya-san sarcastically commented, "It tastes like the bottom of a garbage can," so I dropped the scones . . . b-but I can't give the project up now. And Kiriya-san should be more tactful. His blunt-selfish character is just too much. He's been really cold, especially toward me. Every time he's received a tip from a female customer, he's faced me and thumbed his nose at me.

Argh, he's too blunt! If he continues to ridicule his fellow maids, Allah, Buddha, and the Maid God will punish him for sure! I hope the au gratin dish blows up in Kiriya-san's face, causing him to flail about, trip over his feet, dive face-first into a cabinet, wobble out into the streets, seeking help, and get run over by a two-ton truck . . . a fitting retribution! I've had enough of his arrogance!

Pardon me for venting. But Kiriya-san's snotty attitude has been going way overboard. Not only has he been giving attitude to fellow maids, but he's also rude to customers.

Everyone, do you remember Ozuma-san? The man who gave me a Steiff Teddy Bear during my rookie year?

The other day, Ozuma-san returned to our café.

It was 2 P.M., when the café had slowed down after the lunch rush. I was trying to carry a large pile of dirty dishes back to the kitchen when Ozuma-san entered through the door. It was so sudden that I almost forgot to say, "Welcome home!" Ozuma-san looked at me, and sat down at his usual table near the entrance.

"Long time no see."

"Welcome home, Ozuma-san! I haven't seen you in a long time!"

"You remember me?"

"Of course! I kept the teddy you gave me at this café. And since then, I've sold *doujinshi* at the Comiket, interviewed new employees, and even became a producer to set up a new Events Day. . . ."

"You've become quite proficient."

"Huh? What do you mean?"

"That."

Ozuma-san pointed to the pile of dirty dishes I carried with both arms.

"You would have dropped those back then."

"Y-Yes! I worked hard to get better! Oh, you want coffee, right? I'll bring it right away!"

Oh gosh, I couldn't stop smiling after being complimented so much. I was really giddy as I washed the dishes and poured the coffee. *Tsk,* I want Ozuma-san to go to heaven with my wonderful coffee, packed with my efforts of enduring rigorous maid training to become a top-notch maid. Please savor the fruits of my labor and rise up to heaven . . . whoa!

"I'll take it," Kiriya-san said.

He loomed over and stole the cup of coffee from me.

"No, Kiriya-san, maids should serve male Masters, and Ozuma-san is my—"

"I'll do it," Kiriya-san interjected.

He snagged the cup of coffee from above and walked

straight toward Ozuma-san. Gosh! He's so rude! I thought. It's his fault that the café's quality of service dropped. While it's true that the tip system raised profits temporarily, if this bad service continues, we will gradually lose our regular customers. . . . Hmm, what's that?

Kiriya-san and Ozuma-san were staring at each other. It almost looked like sparks were flying between them. The other customers sensed the eerie tension. Wh-What was going on? It looked like they were talking, but their voices were too low for me to hear. Regardless of the conversation, it wasn't good to have Kiriya-san staring down a Master like a roughneck gangster from Ibaraki Prefecture. I rushed over to him.

"Kiriya-san! Please serve the coffee to the Master immediately!"

"Whatever."

Kiriya-san clicked his tongue, placed the coffee tray on the table, and left. Gosh, what was wrong with him? I wished he'd stop acting so rude. Why was Kiriya-san antagonizing Ozuma-san?

Don't tell me he got the wrong idea when he saw me talking to Ozuma-san! Was the stare Kiriya-san's way of displaying jealousy, like something from a love comedy? I'd rather marry a bombardier beetle (stink bug) than go out with Kiriya-san, but he did express his love for me, so he's probably jealous of Ozuma-san.

"You're having a hard time, Aaliyah-san."

"Oh no! I mean, I'm sorry! I apologize for our waiter's rudeness! . . . Umm, Ozuma-san, the coffee is still hot."

"Thank you for the coffee."

Ozuma-san gulped down the coffee, paid the bill, and left. We'd probably gotten him upset.

After closing . . .

I took off my white brim and slumped onto the table. It was an overly exhausting day, but I couldn't go to sleep just yet. I had less than a week before the Victorian Café Events Day. The interior designs, maid outfits, and china were set, but I still had to find a special dessert for the event. My scones were trashed, so, umm, I wanted something special. . . .

"Hey, there," Ruruka-san said, as she entered the break room.

Her face was a little paler than usual from the relentless work pace. Actually, her face looked more gloomy than pale. Even if she is a mysterious character, as a maid she shouldn't have a gloomy face. It'll just tire her out more. "Hey! How about a dessert in Ruruka-san's image, like the Jack the Ripper Bloody Strawberry Crepe or the Divine Revelation from Outer Space Cheesecake!" I said.

"Maybe," Ruruka-san replied nonchalantly as she toyed with her cell phone.

What was wrong with her? According to the rank chart, she was second from the bottom, but I didn't think she cared about it much. But she had such a sad face!

"You should smile from ear to ear, and be the mysterious extraterrestrial girl you always are, Ruruka-san!"

Ruruka-san sighed deeply and said, "Hey, you're missing the point."

Eh . . . ?

"You need to read between the lines. You say 'maid' so often, it's annoying."

Ruruka-san was getting ready to go home. I stood stock still, not knowing how to react to Ruruka-san's unusually irate response. The Ruruka-san I knew was usually really mysterious, out in space, telling fortunes, predicting that evil monsters will destroy Tokyo, and chasing after supposedly supernatural beings with her eyes . . . !

Ruruka-san changed out of her maid outfit and left the break room. She looked at me with a troubled expression and sighed, "Don't you know how to establish a character?"

She turned around and muttered "Good night" as she left. I could only stare at her back as she disappeared. Her comments, mixing criticism with plain disappointment, left me speechless.

Unsure of what to do next, I went to the corner of the break room and hugged Major Lawrence.

Major Lawrence stared back with his big, black eyes. I felt his gentle gaze on me while I held him close.

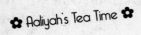
❀ Aaliyah's Tea Time ❀

March 18   **A Master dropping by**

Aaliyah-san, are you still alive . . . ?

March 18   **A Master dropping by**

I guess you're too busy to respond.

15
Spinning Victorian Café

Watch a super-maid in action! One round teaspoon for orange pekoe and flower tea, and half a teaspoon for milk tea. In order to bring out the flavor and aroma, pour at least two cups at once. The pot and cups should be pre-warmed, and once the tea leaves are inserted, pour in the hot water. Once the pot is filled with hot water, wait a specified time for each type of tea. Please be careful not to leave the tea leaves in too long because they'll become bitter. Once the tea is ready, pour the tea into the cups using a strainer. For milk teas, the milk should be in the cup before the tea.

"Why are you smiling while you're pouring tea?" asked Yukino-san.

"*Tsk,* Yukino-san. What do you think of my tea-serving skills? I'm doing it so well that I want to pat myself on the back. I've researched and practiced so hard, and hope my tea-serving skills will impress an English lady so much that while she won't throw out her umbrella, she'll definitely run out of her house barefooted. I've got it down pat. I can now defeat *Kamen no Maid Guy* and *Emma* with my skills!"

"That's nice," Yukino-san mumbled as she walked away.

I didn't have time to respond to her because I was busy going over things before the café opened.

The café had been transformed into a members-only nineteenth-century Victorian Era café. We had a butler, a footman, and maids in colorful apron dresses. The soft glowing lamps provided a soft ambience inside. *Would you like some lemonade or strawberry ice cream?* (Information printed on the Victorian Café flyer.)

Yes, today was the first day of my first project, the Victorian Café!

The days leading up to the opening were hard and long. But look! (Well, you probably can't, but . . .) I used Buckingham Palace and members-only clubs as models to decorate our nineteenth-century British café. The café interior was set with William Morris (like) tables, with a Mintons tea set (sort of), and a Gillows cabinet (or something similar to it). We took Major Lawrence out of the break room and had him sit in the main hall as part of the decorations.

Of course, the maids weren't just "maids." We split them up into different roles, just like the British royalty and nobles did. Let me introduce them to you, one by one!

"If we don't make enough to cover the project costs . . . we'll just sell Aaliyah-chan ★," by Makoto-tencho.

Shiver shiver . . . the housekeeper, in charge of all the maids, was Makoto-tencho, of course. She used the carrot-and-stick method to discipline maids, and her special skill was to force maids to work the "dreamy, magical overtime." I tried to emulate the old ways by calling her "Mrs.

Makoto" but she gave me the most wicked smile on Earth. Her icy glare could wipe out the whole human race.

"Double-check everything. Aaliyah needs to triple-check, though," said Yukino.

The footman, a handsome servant who greeted customers at the door, was none other than Yukino-san. She wore a classy gentleman's suit. When I said, "This role is known for being peacock-like. Please do your best as a peacock, Yukino-san!" she gave me the most horrifying look ever. It was like Medusa's gaze that turned people into stone. Shiver shiver . . .

"If I die . . . I guess nobody can replace me," by Ruruka-san.

The parlor maid (ballroom staff) was Ruruka-san. Her outfit was more colorful and entertaining than plain maid outfits that were used for normal duties. By Victorian standards, a woman with white, pale skin (sickly beauty) was considered beautiful, so Ruruka-san fit the bill perfectly. But beware . . . she might utter unfound prophecies, look thunderstruck, and proclaim, "The savior of the world has been born!" as if she was conversing with God. She wasn't a "sickly beauty," but rather, just "sick"!

"You chose these dishes, Aaliyah-san? They're so lame."

The butler, in charge of all the servants alongside the housekeeper, was Kiriya-san. He was blunt-selfish as usual, but I suppose a slightly mean butler probably existed back then, so I let it slide. I wasn't sure how to answer him when he asked, "Where is the silverware? Polishing silverware is one of a butler's duties."

"If you have to polish something, then use sandpaper to polish a *Ganpura*!"

Finally, the house maid, wearing a plain maid outfit, was me, Aaliyah Kominami, completing the Victorian Café ensemble. For the next week, our café would time-travel back to nineteenth-century England. Fortunately, the tip system was on hold during this event.

Did everyone notice my glow? I'm only an inch away from becoming the ultimate maid . . . no, I might have reached the top of the maid mountain already. Dinner rolls, muffins, pound cakes, plum cakes, and biscuits were fully stocked. We were ready to welcome the Masters now . . . !

"Aaliyah-san, stop grinning and get ready," said Kiriya-san.

Oh, yes, the café was about to open! And Kiriya-san's friends reserved the café this morning. It's unusual to reserve the first half of the day during an Events Day, but it's easier to manage a known number of reservation customers than an overflow of customers rushing in. The café would open to regular customers during the afternoon. I couldn't wait to change into the afternoon maid outfit!

"Time to open!"

At 10 A.M. sharp, the maids lined up at the entrance and stood by for our Masters. Kiriya-san opened the door. The customers who reserved the café entered.

"Welcome to our Victorian Era café, Masters!"

". . . What?"

Large men in black suits entered through the door Kiriya-san opened. There were four of them. They stomped the floors, bumped shoulders, and glared at everyone. They seemed to know the café's layout because one man stood in front of each exit.

The fresh start of our café suddenly went cold and slippery, like Jell-O.

All the maids were rendered speechless. We stood in place, unable to understand the surprising turn of events.

Except Kiriya-san, that is.

"Playtime is over," he said.

His cold voice sounded sinister. While the men in black guarded the exits, Kiriya-san tossed aside his coat and tie and leaned back into the sofa.

"Why does someone of your status want to be a servant so much?" Kiriya-san asked me. His eyes were locked on me, full of seriousness. The other maids turned to look at me, too. I tried to step back, but after two steps, a table blocked my way. The tea set clanked at the light impact.

"Let's return to your country. You need to fulfill the contract."

Kiriya-san's chilling comments cut right through me. The men in black displayed no emotions.

"Kiriya-san, what are you saying? And what are you doing? I refuse to listen to your demands. Why are you saying such crazy things, Kiriya-san . . . ?"

"Yukino-san, you've been suspicious, haven't you?" Kiriya-san inquired.

I didn't care if he insulted me, but not the other maids. Regardless, he continued to tell his version of the "truth" to them.

"She's hiding her true identity," declared Kiriya-san.

The other maids focused on me. I looked down at the floor, trying to deny the storm that was about to start.

"Please don't look at me like that. You're telling such a preposterous story, no one will believe you. Kiriya-san made all this up. It's a very bad joke. It's all a lie!"

"In Swahili, 'Aaliyah' means 'the exalted one.' She chose 'Aaliyah' because she is truly the exalted one." Kiriya-san huffed and crossed his legs. He seemed overconfident and conceited.

"You don't have to believe me. I don't care if you think I'm a crazy psychopath saying incomprehensible things. Even I can't believe that someone of nobility is working as a servant, for Christ's sake."

Kiriya-san stood up and slowly walked toward me. I tried to back away, but the table was in the way.

"Let's return. Now. Quit dreaming. I'll take you home whether you like it or not."

"No. No! I want to stay here! I want to work here as a maid!"

But Kiriya-san continued to close in on me. My knees shook so badly I couldn't move away. My teeth chattered violently. Kiriya-san reached out and grabbed my arm. . . .

But the very next moment, there was a tremendous *thud*, and one of the men guarding the doors fell forward.

Everyone turned in response to the sound.

"Aaliyah-san, this way. Hurry!" Ozuma-san yelled.

Ozuma-san stood in the opening. He stepped over the fallen man and waved me out of the café. I furiously shook off Kiriya-san's hand and darted away. Another black-suited man tried to stop me, but Ozuma-san shielded me as I bolted from the café.

I ran into the crowded streets of Akihabara in my maid outfit.

. . . And left my beloved place of employment.

16

Can I Wear a Maid Outfit?

This is a story about a country far, far away.

Of course, you can ignore this story if you want. Or think of it as a piece of fiction. If you can at least acknowledge that it could be possible, that's all I ask of you. It's trivial knowledge, really.

There was a small, distant kingdom with a long history. The royal family acted more like figureheads, holding some final authority, while most matters were decided by the federal council. But the royal family was considered the main symbol of the country and was widely admired by the citizenry.

A certain conglomerate, partnered with many large companies, became interested in the country.

Are you aware of the phrase "industrial colonialism"? It is one of the methods an industry uses to take over or monopolize a nation's economy. First, a large company will introduce a large number of factories with a lot of expensive equipment to mass-produce products, raising the quality of goods. Small- and mid-sized companies will not be able to keep up with the mass production and expensive machinery costs, and eventually lose out to the large conglomerate. The country will gradually lose its rich history and traditions under the conglomerate's "globalization" strategies.

It was only a matter of time before this country devolved into an industrial colony. The royal family, stripped of all authority, tried in vain to resist the conglomerate. But the conglomerate worked its influence into the federal council and applied political pressure. It evolved into a battle between the royal family and the conglomerate.

Amid the chaos, the conglomerate members laid their eyes on the princess. They plotted to have a conglomerate executive marry into the royal family. The royal family was only a figurehead, but if the marriage went through, the people would believe that the royal family officially endorsed the conglomerate. It would mark the defeat of the royal family. It would take time, but the conglomerate would eventually take over the whole nation.

But the princess ran away.

The princess escaped to the Far East and worked in a small café. She finally obtained a life of her own choosing. She didn't want to become a princess of a kingdom, but rather, dreamed of becoming a waitress in a small café. Of course, it didn't take long for someone to discover her whereabouts. That someone was the royal family's agent, sent to confirm her presence and protect her as necessary.

But why didn't the agent bring her back to her country?

For the royal family, it was best not to have the princess in the country. Without the princess, there would be no marriage.

But the conglomerate also found her, and began to pressure her. They didn't resort to violence at first, though. One would think they'd have sent a conglomerate pawn into the café to harass her, but in reality the conglomerate was bold enough to send in the executive suitor who was to marry the princess. The suitor chipped away at the princess little by little, and eventually proposed to her. But the princess refused, frustrating the suitor. He continued to make her life miserable.

Once the suitor lost his patience, though, he took harsher actions. He planned to ruin the princess at the peak of her happiness, and tried to drag her back to her country. Thanks to the royal family's agent, though, the princess was able to slip away, but she and the agent couldn't return to the café and didn't know where to go next.

I repeat . . . this is trivial knowledge . . . because saving my country was secondary. I wanted to personally work in Akihabara. I wanted to do a job that provided comfort to people. I chased my fantasies and ran off to Japan. That's all.

I knew Yukino-san had her suspicions. I also knew Ozuma-san's true identity. As Ruruka-san stated, I might have been in over my head. I refused to acknowledge reality, chased after my dreams, and indulged in my fantasies.

We eventually reached the Mansei Bridge. The water underneath flowed gently, unaffected by the excitement above. The clear, bright skies complemented the glitter of the sunshine on the calm, clear water surface.

A cold voice from the rear sent chills down my back.

"It's useless. Give up," Kiriya-san growled.

"I'm a maid. I'm a maid in Akihabara. I just want to work hard every day."

"We just want to introduce cheap items into your country's market. We call that 'industrial development,' you know. We're trying to do what's best for your country."

"To provide a comforting, relaxing atmosphere . . . that's our mission . . . no, our pleasure!" I yelled.

"Stop being so childish. Wait, you're only fifteen, aren't you? I guess you're still a kid after all."

I didn't reply.

Was this the end?

Looking back, all I did was make life harder for the other maids. Yukino-san tried so hard to teach me basic maid skills, but I was still a no-good maid. I was never able to share my feelings with Ruruka-san even at the end. I wasn't able to apologize to Makoto-tencho for ruining our Events Day.

I had no place to turn.

My fantasy was over.

"Okay. I'll go back home."

"Good," said Kiriya-san. He sarcastically clapped.

"It's about time. I can buy anything for your happiness."

Kiriya-san slowly approached me. He reached out with his hand. No matter how much I detested it, I'd probably have to take this man's hand and return to my country. For the sake of the country and its people. I had to live my life for others and face reality. . . .

As Kiriya-san sported his wicked smile, a familiar set of arm cuffs wrapped around his hips.

"It's time for a swim! You horrible Master!" the voice said.

The cuffed arms locked around Kiriya-san's midriff and her heel swept Kiriya-san's ankles to topple him over the bridge. . . .

Splash!

Kiriya-san was thrown into the Kanda River.

"You're still on shift, aren't you? You're not allowed to leave like that," Yukino-san said as she turned around, her tailcoat fluttering. Despite her harsh warning, she was smiling.

"Here, Aaliyah-chan," Makoto-tencho said.

I just stood there flabbergasted. I felt a pile of sticks placed in my hand. Makoto-tencho handed me a stack of bottle rockets.

"Umm, Makoto-tencho, where did you get these?"

". . . Just fire them," said Ruruka-san.

She pulled my hand over to the bridge railing. Kiriya-san was struggling to stay afloat, spouting incomprehensible words and trying to swim toward the riverbank. Ruruka-san pointed a handful of bottle rockets toward Kiriya-san and lit the fuses.

Pop, po-pop! Po-po-po-pop!

"*Glurg* . . . stop . . . oww . . . hey! *Glubb* . . . !?"

Kiriya-san freaked out at the bottle rocket attacks and bobbed up and down. He didn't seem like a good swimmer. He flailed his arms and legs, but it only caused him to drift away from the edge. The bottle rockets whistled, popped on the water, and fizzled.

"Here, fire away," ordered Ruruka-san.

Ruruka-san handed me a lighter to light my bottle rockets.

"But . . . if I do this, I'll just make more trouble for everyone! I lied to everyone! I was running away from reality. I really appreciate everyone's help, but I can't involve everyone in my mess. You don't have to stay. Please leave me alone!"

Yukino-san shook her head and ignored my pleas.

"Ozuma-san . . . or whatever his real name might be . . . told us everything," Ruruka-san said.

"Then you know you shouldn't get involved! You should know what you're up against!"

"It's okay. We need a dreamer like you. You might as well dream all the way to the end. Besides, you care about our café the most. What is the café going to do without you?" Ruruka-san added.

"B-But . . ."

"Stop whining! What's the eleventh cardinal rule of maids?" Yukino-san suddenly asked.

"Yes! Maids aren't allowed to leave their place of duty without authorization!"

Yukino-san chuckled at my automatic recital of the rule and said, "It is the senior maid's duty to educate and discipline no-good junior maids."

"But I hid the truth from everyone. You'll probably never forgive me! And I've been making everyone mad. . . ."

"We're not mad," Ruruka-san replied.

She looked me straight in the eye. Her usually pale, sullen face was now glowing pink with life.

"Still, I feel so bad for causing trouble. . . ."

"We're not mad."

"But . . ."

"We're not mad, okay? I-I was just worried about you the other day!"

I started laughing.

"What's so funny?!"

"I'm sorry . . . Ruruka-san . . . you act like a mystery girl, but you're actually a *tsundere*!"

"I am not! No way!" Ruruka-san blushed as she turned away.

Yukino-san, Makoto-tencho, and I couldn't stop smiling at her adorable reactions.

I felt a warm, fuzzy feeling blossom inside.

I took Ruruka-san's lighter, aimed the bottle rockets at Kiriya-san, and fired the rockets.

Whiss-whiss-whiss-whiss . . . Po-po-po-po-po-po-po-pop!

"*Ugg . . . glugg . . .* how dare you . . . *glurb!*"

Every time a bottle rocket popped, Kiriya-san's head bobbed in and out of the water. Each pop released the darkness festering in my heart, and I eventually felt refreshed. Yes, as long as my coworkers, café, and customers need me, I won't cry or return to my country . . . !

"I never thought these firecrackers would come in handy," Yukino-san remarked.

"When she bought all of these firecrackers for our *yukata* event, I thought of firing her," Makoto-tencho lamented.

"She even bought a string-shaped firecracker . . ." Ruruka-san complained.

I tried to ignore their scary conversation in the background and focused on the battle instead. Kiriya-san was completely drowning at this point.

"This is the final blow," said Makoto-tencho, as she tossed me a huge cherry bomb cannon that I could barely wrap my arm around. I recognized this piece because I had bought this hazardous weapon during my rookie year. Acting as if I was seeing it for the very first time, I pulled up the opening of the tube over my head. Ruruka-san lit the fuse wire.

"Kiriya-san, please rise up to heaven on an express escalator. This is my first and final service to you. Please be so gracious as to accept . . . *a maid's anger*!"

Ka-boom!

The cherry bomb blasted the water surface with a bang. A pillar of water and ear-splitting sound muffled Kiriya-san's screams as he sank underwater. We all breathed a sigh of relief and watched the water rippling over him.

"Let's run away," Makoto-tencho said, as she pulled my sleeve.

I suppose it goes without saying that we'd attracted a lot of attention. We were totally surrounded by curious onlookers. With Yukino-san leading, we broke through the crowds and ran off into Akihabara's main strip.

"B-But aren't the men in black still at the café? What should we do?"

"Oh shoot, you're right," said Makoto-tencho.

Makoto-tencho was so sloppy at times. If we returned to the café without a plan, we'd jump right into the lion's mouth. Even though we'd gotten rid of Kiriya-san, the men in black still awaited us at the café. And even if we got rid of them too, it was only a temporary solution at best. We needed a plan to stop Kiriya-san's group from taking over.

At that moment, a figure between the buildings jumped out. Yukino-san stopped in her tracks. She postured herself to defend. . . .

"I'm sorry for being late."

"Ozuma-san! You made it out okay!"

As Ozuma-san dusted off his clothes, he replied, "Yes." He had an ugly bruise on his left cheek, but he was ignoring his pain.

Ozuma-san said, completely poker-faced, "I have a plan. It requires everyone's assistance."

Akihabara's Sky Is Forever Blue

We slipped into a dark alley and tried to be inconspicuous. The dark passageway I had just ignored every day turned out to be damp and cold. We had to remain hidden until our plan was executed.

I breathed in, and breathed out. A simple procedure, but it calmed me down.

The next moment, I heard a cherry bomb explode inside the café.

The apron and dress were considered to be a maid's "battle uniform." I couldn't have agreed more. I gripped the machinegun handle so hard that my nails went white.

Ozuma-san asked, "The doll is in the café, correct?"

Why did he ask me that?

"You mean Major Lawrence, the Steiff Teddy Bear? Of course it's sitting in the café, but why do you ask?"

"I put a recorder inside it."

". . . Whaat? A recorder, as in . . . a bug?"

"Yes, I suppose."

O-Oh my gosh. If I had taken Major Lawrence home instead of leaving him at the café, my private life would have been wide open for Ozuma-san's listening pleasure!

"It should have recorded Kiriya-san's voice when he revealed his plans at the café. That recording can be used as evidence to convict him. We can nullify his conglomerate's plan. Oh . . . I apologize for deceiving you."

"No, don't worry about it. You had to conceal our identity because of your job."

"Actually, it's Aaliyah's fault for accepting the gift without suspecting anything," Yukino-san criticized.

"Didn't I tell you to always inspect all gifts from customers? There are times when something is embedded," Makoto-tencho warned.

"I knew about it . . . but I thought it'd be fun to keep it there," Ruruka-san snickered.

"Gosh, why didn't you tell me, Ruruka-san? And stop laughing, Ozuma-san. Let's execute this plan before I make more mistakes . . . er, I mean, before the situation worsens! Ozuma-san, where is the recording device located?" I said.

"It's placed inside the doll itself."

"You don't have an external device that saves data from the doll?"

"To be more accurate, it's not really a bug. It isn't proper to listen to Aaliyah-san's private conversations. It was only for emergency situations. The device is activated by sound, and can only retain the last five hours of data."

"So we can't wait until everything settles before we retrieve it?"

"Exactly. By then, Kiriya-san's threats will have been automatically erased. Our time limit is four hours. If we don't retrieve the doll by then, the data will be lost forever."

"Gosh, this is going to be tough. We need to fight through those big guards and retrieve Major Lawrence. . . . It's mission impossible!"

"But once we obtain the voice data, we can end this once and for all. We *must* succeed."

"Ozuma-san, I'm really afraid to ask this question . . . but what will happen if we can't obtain the data?"

"You'll have to return to your country, Aaliyah-san. And I don't know what will happen to the café."

My one-piece dress and apron fluttered in the wind as I dashed toward the café. I had to sneak in through the rear entrance and retrieve Major Lawrence.

"I'm sorry, but I need to have Aaliyah-san in the safest position. It's my job to do so," Ozuma-san strongly but apologetically requested. Our plan was as follows: Ozuma-san would lead the group as they burst in through the front entrance, pinning the men in black. I would slip in through the back entrance to retrieve Major Lawrence.

"This simple plan might work, but I'm worried about everyone else being harmed. I feel bad for having the safest role."

"There's no other choice, Aaliyah," Yukino-san said.

"Besides, you're Aaliyah . . ." Makoto-tencho added.

". . . The no-good maid," Ruruka-san piped in.

I didn't know if they were trying to hide their embarrassment, but their comments almost made tears well up in my eyes. Even a maid sheds tears.

"If we make it out of this alive, I'll feed my homemade scones to all of you until your bellies burst!"

"Hell no!" they all replied in unison.

"You didn't have to go stereo on me. Nice senior maids, indeed!"

"Aaliyah-san, take this."

Ozuma-san put a machinegun in my hand. Of course, not a real one . . . an altered air submachinegun. But the black, gleaming metal and slightly heavy body felt real enough in my hand. Just a few more feet till I reached the rear entrance.

Although I'm sure the men in black wouldn't feel threatened by girly maids, if I wasted too much time, with every minute my colleagues would be exposed to more and more danger. I threw open the door and jumped into the break room.

I heard a lot of crashing noises from the other side of the door. The blocking operation was in full effect. I had to retrieve Major Lawrence immediately and give everyone a chance to retreat—their efforts would prove fruitless if I got caught. I had to be swift and silent. In order to successfully accomplish this mission, I needed the maid skills to emulate an invisible fairy.

Although I'd opened this door millions of times, it somehow felt like a heavy iron gate this time. I twisted the doorknob silently, swallowed my breath, and mustered enough courage to enter.

The café looked like a typhoon-stricken area.

Ozuma-san and the maids were engaging the men in

black. One of the men noticed me, but the maids threw things at him nonstop, halting him in his tracks. If the blocking operation continued successfully, I was supposed to run out of the front entrance and blend into the crowded streets of Akihabara. At this rate, we might actually knock the men out. Anyway, I had to retrieve Major Lawrence!

Major Lawrence was sitting on top of the light brown cabinet. I ran over and hugged him.

"I've retrieved the data, everyone! Please get out of—"

"Aaliyah, behind you!" Yukino-san yelled. I immediately dived to the floor. A police baton swatted the air above me.

"You're not going anywhere . . ." said Kiriya-san, standing there with water dripping off his hair and clothes. He no longer had the luxury of acting conceited and instead looked rather sinister. "Stay where you are!"

I pointed my machinegun at him.

"Oww!" Kiriya-san winced in pain, but it only stopped him momentarily. I tried to aim for his face, but the recoil pushed my string of bullets upward. The first shot grazed the top of his head but the rest hit the wall above him. Kiriya-san regained his posture and closed in for a second attack before I could pull the trigger again. As he tried to swing the baton down, I instinctively raised both hands to block it. He struck the machinegun out of my hand.

"Gotcha!"

Kiriya-san grabbed my collar and pushed me into the cabinet, and the doors rattled. I tried to fish for a weapon, but all I felt was the smooth cabinet surface.

I felt Kiriya-san's breath on my face. His bloodshot eyes

were burning with rage. "Why are you taking care of god-damn strangers? Look at you. You can't even save *yourself*."

Kiriya-san raised his baton. Ozuma-san and the maids couldn't help me now because they were occupied with their own battles. I tried to break free from his grip, but all I could do was feel the cabinet doors. My fate was about to reach a terrible climax.

Although I had come this far, this was truly the end. My short time at the café flashed before my eyes. The Victorian Café had never really come to be. My efforts of picking out the right desserts and teas, making maid outfits, and polishing the china . . . it had all been wasted.

During the flashbacks, my body reacted instinctively. My hands moved automatically, repeating the procedure I'd done a billion times. I opened the cabinet door silently, pulled out a teapot, and . . .

"What the . . . !"

Kiriya-san tried to stop me by swinging his baton down.

Almost simultaneously—no, one-tenth of a second faster—my teapot smacked Kiriya-san's left temple.

The impact made a loud crash that echoed throughout the room.

Amid the airborne fragments of the smashed teapot, Kiriya-san slowly fell to the floor. He stretched out on the floor, moaning.

As I looked down on the unconscious Kiriya-san, I dusted off my apron dress. I had mixed feelings toward him. I tried to find words to describe them, in vain. I didn't know any complicated words, and I guess it was pointless anyway to describe how I felt at that point. But one thing was for certain. I wanted to tell my former co-worker, Kiriya-san, one thing. . . .

"By serving others, you save yourself. Even if it's a dream, it's a nice dream to have."

I picked up my white brim and positioned it back on my head.

". . . Practice and review. It's the quickest path to improvement."

I recalled a senior maid ingraining that into my head.

My senior maids peered into the oven, which were full of freshly baked scones. A really suspicious face, next to an ambiguously smiling face, next an expressionless face. They stared at the tray of scones I pulled from the oven. Reluctantly, the three hands reached out. . . .

"You should shorten the baking time," Yukino-san remarked.

"Tastes good," Makoto-tencho complimented.

"It's edible but boring. Add habanero sauce to spice things up," Ruruka-san suggested.

"Does that mean it passes the test? Or did it fail again? Umm, well, I'm afraid, but please raise your O and X signs. . . ."

Yukino-san advised, "If you're making another batch, it needs to taste better." (X)

Makoto-tencho lamented, "It costs too much." (X)

Ruruka-san quizzically answered, "Triangle. Or square?" (TRIANGLE or SQUARE?)

My senior maids had totally criticized me again. "Gosh! Then I'll just have to get better! Fine. One day, I'll make scones so delicious that all of you will throw your bodies to the ground and chant, 'Oh, beautiful Aaliyah, please sell your scones in our café, we beg of you!' Just watch me."

I pouted as I swept the main hall before opening the café. Most of the furniture in the café had needed only minor repairs and was still usable. Major Lawrence, who had been gutted (to remove the recording device), was sewn back up, with the help of Ruruka-san's ultimate (umm, yeah, right) evil sewing skills. Our break room mascot now decorated the café interior. I wiped Major Lawrence with a damp rag and polished his big, black eyes. I polished the water glasses and prepared the tea sets. I was ready to serve delicious teas from around the world!

Clang clang.

Oh, the café just opened its doors.

Under the skies of Akihabara, the Masters have "come home" to their favorite maid cafés.

"Welcome home, Master!"

Hmm, this is odd.

We're missing some silverware.

I don't know where it went.

Silver-ware?

I'll ask people in the order of suspicion!

Big trouble! It's a crisis for our café!

Aaliyah, the super-maid, must solve this problem!

Okay!

I can't eat metal!

No!

In your sleep?

Did you eat some, Aaliyah?

Suzuhito Yasuda   The Melancholy of a Super-Maid

No, I didn't!

Did you eat it?

Why do you characterize me like that!

Huh? We don't know.

Next, these two.

It's good for her to be serious. Last night, she stayed back and did something in the storage room.

Oh yeah...

She takes things too seriously, so don't tease her too much.

BA-TAM

Same to you, Makoto-tencho.

Fine! I'll go buy some more!

POUT POUT

Oh my.

I'll dock her pay.

She was practicing maid self-defense skills. She was looking for weapons besides firearms.

GA-CHAK

Comicalized by Suzuhito Yasuda

Glossary

Adventure Ranger *Boukengers*. A play on the idea of the Power Rangers. *Bouken* means "journey" or "adventure," so the literal translation of *Boukengers* is "Adventure (Ran)gers."

Akiba. A nickname for Akihabara, a neighborhood in Tokyo that's much frequented by *otaku*, or extreme fanboys. In Akiba, you'll find many anime/manga and electronics shops—and, of course, maid cafés.

Amaterasu Oomikami. In traditional Japanese mythology, the sun goddess.

Area 88, Pineapple Army. *Area 88* and *Pineapple Army* are famous anime and manga titles. In the anime and manga *Area 88*, Shin Kazama is an ace pilot who's tricked into signing a three-year contract with a foreign mercenary aviation unit. In the manga *Pineapple Army*, a former U.S. Marine trains his clients in self-defense using military techniques.

Boys Love (BL) *doujinshi*. Gay love stories, often depicting *bishônen* (pretty boys). In the book, instead of using the terms "BL" or "yaoi," Aaliyah preferred to use her own phrase, "homo manga," but the word "homo" has negative connotations in English. Because "homo" doesn't sound degrading in Japanese (no negative implications), it was translated into English using the softer phrase, "gay love manga," or "gay manga."

Computer chat icons. Throughout the text, you'll notice a number of familiar emoticons or computer chat icons. These were adapted from Japanese computer chat icons, most of which are similar to American chat icons. Below are the icons often used in this book. Because the "laugh" icon used a Japanese kanji for "laugh" between the parentheses (笑), "LOL" was used as a substitute.

   ^_^ = smile
   T_T = cry
   >_< = frustrated

Cosplayer. Cosplay is short for "costume play." One can cosplay by dressing up as a fictional character or celebrity or by putting on any elaborate, fanciful costume—such as a traditional maid's uniform.

Dazai, Osamu. Early twentieth-century Japanese novelist.

Dhalsim, Yoga Fire, and Dragon Punch. Dhalsim is a character from the Street Fighter II video game; Yoga Fire and Dragon Punch are some attack moves from the same game.

Doujinshi. Self-published comic/manga. Ranges from original amateur/professional works to fan-fiction. Some *doujinshi* artists draw overtly pornographic stories, sometimes featuring well-known characters from anime and manga.

Doutor. A major coffee shop chain in Japan, rivaling Starbucks in ubiquity.

EOCS. Ethics Organization of Computer Software. Organization that urged software game makers to put "18+ (Adults only)" ratings on their games. As with JARO, Aaliyah thought of the wrong organization to deal with her labor-related complaints.

Food tickets. Many Japanese restaurants, usually small, put up a vending machine with preset menu items at the front of their store. Customers can then purchase the ticket of the dish they want, hand it to the store worker, and seat themselves as they wait for their order. This process eliminated the wait time during which customers are deciding what to order.

Ganpura. An abbreviation referring to a plastic model kit based on the popular Gundam anime franchise. Gundam model kits have long been known for their extreme detailing and their cult of devotees.

Goth-Loli. Short for "Gothic Lolita," a trendy style of dress among young Japanese women. The style combines elaborate, Victorian-style dresses—complete with bonnets and petticoats, and in styles originally intended for very young girls—with elements popularized by the Goth subculture, such as black velvet, coffin-shaped handbags, and other morbid accoutrements.

Hell Teacher Nube. A Japanese manga title. The main character is an elementary school teacher who uses his demon hand to protect his students from evil monsters and spirits.

Holori and *polori. Holori* (or *horori*) is a sound word often used in manga to describe a teardrop rolling down the cheek. Thus the phrase "*Holori to shite shimau hanashi*" meant "a touching story that brings tears to your eyes." *Polori,* on the other hand, is a sound effect from manga used to describe something bouncing/popping out (i.e., exposed breasts), with heavy sexual connotations. Thus, the Master (assumed to be a male) seemed slightly embarrassed and hesitant to correct Aaliyah (a female) on the misuse of the word "*polori.*" And upon reflection, it embarrassed Aaliyah as well.

Ikebukuro's Otome Road. If Akihabara is considered to be a male *otaku*'s town, then Otome (Maiden) Road, right out of Tokyo's Ikebukuro Station East Exit, is the female *otaku* equivalent. Many anime and manga shops on Otome Road sell products aimed at the female audience, such as yaoi.

JARO. Japan Advertisement Review Organization. Reviews TV commercials/ads, and receives complaints from consumers regarding false/inaccurate advertisements. Commercials spots in which JARO solicits complaints (regarding ads) are so common that many Japanese have the mistaken belief that JARO will listen to all complaints, even those having nothing to do with advertisements, just as Aaliyah does.

Megiddo Flame. References a name of an extremely powerful attack in video games like Final Fantasy VIII and X, among others, rather than to the actual Megiddo in Israel, the site of Armageddon.

Moe. An otaku term meaning "cute, charming, adorable, or sweet." Typically used to describe adorable girls who show extreme cuteness through appearance, speech, or behavior.

Omu-rice. Short for "omelet-rice," a common Japanese dish. It consists of an omelet with fried rice in the middle.

Ossu. Short greeting/pep cheer often grunted by karate/martial artists. Similar to U.S. military grunts "hoo-ah" and "oorah."

Otaku. Generally a term used to describe anime/manga fanatics or "nerds," and more broadly used to describe any sort of fanatic, such as figurine otakus, *Ganpura* otakus, BL otakus, et cetera.

Seirogan. A well-known pill with a distinct, strong smell used to alleviate gastrointestinal ailments. People across the room can smell a bottle of *Seirogan* when opened.

Tencho. Similar to other honorifics such as "-san" or "-sensei," the suffix "-tencho" is used when addressing a store manager.

Tsundere. A portmanteau combining the words *tsun-tsun* (cold, harsh, mean) and *dere-dere* (sweet, kind, loving, affectionate). Typically used to describe girls (and some guys) who are mean, or even violent, to those they love in public, but very affectionate in private. Prominent examples of *tsundere* manga/anime characters include *Naru Narusegawa, Lum,* et cetera. In *Maid Machinegun,* Aaliyah patronizes a *tsundere* café where waitresses specialize in treating customers in *tsundere* fashion.

Uke and *seme.* Terms used to describe which gay character in yaoi is the more passive, or *uke* (receiver), and which is the more aggressive, or *seme* (attacker/aggressor). Based on martial arts terms to describe who initiates the attack (*seme*) and who receives/responds to the attack (*uke*).

Wabi-sabi. *Wabi-sabi* is the Japanese concept of a style of beauty that is "imperfect, impermanent, and incomplete." Aaliyah is saying the difficulty in describing the concept of *wabi-sabi* was similar to explaining why girls love BL manga.

World Maid Guy Tournament. Parody of the World Martial Arts Tournament (*Tenkaichi Budoukai*) in the Dragon Ball manga and anime.

Yakiniku and **shabu-shabu.** *Yakiniku* is grilled meat, and *shabu-shabu* is a hot-pot meat dish in which slices of meat are lightly dunked in a pot of boiling water and dipped in a savory sauce.

Yaoi (801). A more general term for gay love stories, ranging from BL (above) stories that focus on romance to more hard-core, sex-based stories. Yaoi is the shorter form of the phrase "*yama-nashi imi-nashi ochi-nashi,*" or "no climax, no point, no meaning." Each digit of "801" represents each syllable of yaoi (ya = 8, o = 0, i = 1).

Yukata. A light summer kimono.

Zettai Ryoiki. Literally, "a sacred zone." The area of a girl's exposed thigh between a miniskirt and over-the-knee socks. The ideal ratio is 4:1:2.5 (sock-thigh-skirt).

About the Author

Aaliyah is the pseudonym for an author whose true identity has never been released. She came to the attention of the Japanese publishing world when her humorous, diary-style novel *Maid Machinegun* won an online fiction contest sponsored by a literary agency!

About the Illustrator

Suzuhito Yasuda's cute and colorful character designs, sharp linework, and unique design talents have made him a popular artist in the fields of both manga and novel illustration. He has illustrated such Japanese novels as *Kamisama Kazoku, Scarlet Sword,* and *Maid Machinegun.* He is also the creator of the manga series *Yozakura Quartet.*